MOVIE STAR PARKING at the WHITE TOWER

and other stories

MOVIE STAR PARKING at the WHITE TOWER

and other stories

Patrick Halferty

For Beth, who told me to "stop talking and write."

And for my parents, who told me "you'll never know where you're going unless you know where you've been."

Author's Note

The neighborhood of my early life in Pittsburgh was filled with interesting characters, places, and history. Oakland throughout the twentieth century was a microcosm of the Industrial Revolution's influence on many American cities. A diorama, if you will, with steel mills and railroads on one end, and impressive museums, libraries and institutions built by the men who had attained great wealth because of those mills and railroads on the other. In between were immigrant enclaves, churches, shops, restaurants, bars, schools, and all the other things that make the world go 'round. Even a major league ballpark.

The themes of these stories are universal, so you certainly don't have to be familiar with the neighborhood to read them. However, if you do know Pittsburgh and Oakland, then you will recognize some of the streets and places in these pages, and you will also realize that some are fictional. In some stories, it made sense to me to use real landmarks and streets. In others, it was better to use some creative license. Afterall, these are works of fiction, conjured out of my overactive imagination.

Enjoy.

Contents

MOVIE STAR PARKING at the WHITE TOWER

and other stories

Waiting on the Bicycle Boy

"He comes rollin' around the corner on that rickety bicycle like the wind. From the Boulevard all the way out to the Cathedral, and everywhere in between, he delivers the news. Good, bad, or otherwise. Mostly bad, I suppose."

His wide and weathered left hand, minus a little finger thanks to a long-ago accident in the mill, rested on the wooden porch railing as he waved the other towards the intersection.

Thomas Garrett wasn't sure if he was speaking to anyone in particular, but he continued, nonetheless.

"A hell of a thing to put on a kid. A freckle-faced grim reaper. All of fifteen years old."

Sometimes Dorothy Zulenski was on the porch next door. Sometimes she was not. A green canvas awning with thin orange and white stripes separated them. Dorothy was not much for small talk and usually as quiet as a church mouse.

This reticence added to the mystery. He could go on for minutes not knowing whether there was an actual human set of ears on the other end of the conversation. But it made no difference. If he had something to say, he said it. Eventually he would figure out if he had company.

He turned and made his way across the porch, pulling the telegram out of the front pocket of his olive green work pants, taking his usual perch on the glider. He unfolded the dog-eared, yellow sheet and held it at arm's length from his eyes.

"Anyway, I'm sitting right in this very seat and the kid comes 'round the bend, reckless like. I was hoping he'd keep going right by, but something inside me knew where he was headed. There's only Declan and the Italian kid. What's his name? Patsy, from our street overseas. A hell of a thing, to be thinking the worst for some other family. So, the kid nods at me, mumbles something that may have been a hello, hands me the telegram and is gone as quick as he appeared."

Thomas read the telegram aloud for what must have been the fiftieth time in five days. It wasn't necessary. He knew every word by memory.

"THE SECRETARY OF WAR DESIRES ME TO EXPRESS HIS DEEP REGRET THAT YOUR SON PVT. DECLAN GARRETT WAS SERIOUSLY WOUNDED IN FRANCE 10 SEPT 1944."

He looked up at nothing, holding back tears as he continued.

"And so on and so forth. FURTHER INFORMATION TO FOLLOW DIRECT FROM HOSPITAL. Signed, J A ULIO THE ADJUTANT GENERAL."

He meticulously folded the paper and put it in his shirt pocket. Dozens of scenarios had bounced around in his head over the past five days. Some had a happy ending. Most did not. There were few in the middle. Perhaps he will just appear at the front door in a few days, no worse for the wear, in a sling or leaning on a pair of crutches. Or at least he died in a hospital and not alone on a battlefield somewhere in France. That one seemed to scratch its way to the front of his brain the most.

Thomas was no stranger to the darkness of war. In fact, he was well acquainted with the smoky battlefields of France. He knew when Declan left what was in store. It was not glorious, but it was necessary.

"Any word?" Agnes Larkin shook Thomas from his thoughts.

She stood on the sidewalk below, awaiting a response, rosary beads wrapped around the knuckles of her right hand. An umbrella clutched under her left arm, although there was not a cloud in the sky.

"None."

She stood waiting, and he knew she would not budge until he gave her more.

"Same as yesterday, Aggie. And the day before that. I suppose it could be weeks. I heard the baker down on Elsinore Square got bad news straight away. No waiting. I don't know which is worse."

She fixed her gaze on something far away down the block and replied.

"I suppose that depends on the outcome, now, doesn't it? He was a fine young man, the boy from Elsinore Square. I saw his mother on the Boulevard just last month. All smiles. I doubt it will come so easy for her now. Terrible."

Her voice trailed slightly at the end, as if she had caught herself.

"Indeed. Sure, we'll know something soon enough," he said.

Agnes went on her way and Thomas studied the stains at the bottom of his teacup.

He sat alone for what seemed to be five hours. It had been twenty-six minutes. The morning paper would usually help him pass the time away, reading just about every word, front to back. This week he had stayed away from the newspaper and the radio. He was sick and tired of the boastful stories of victories, sad stories of destruction, and endless lists of casualties.

The feeling of being alone was different. He was used to being by himself. This was not the same. There was a loneliness to it. A fear.

***

Years ago, when he was still getting his bearings on American soil, he had noticed her across the floor at an Irish dance at Winebiddle Hall. She was not a classic beauty, but there was something about her. Her amber colored eyes latched on to him that day and never let go. No woman before or after had the same effect on him.

Delia Mary Burke was the youngest of three protective brothers and two incredibly involved sisters from a small village a stone's throw from Lough Nafooey in County Galway. One brother remained in Ireland, but the rest were right here, as if to make sure their baby sister did not go astray. She worked in those days with her sisters as servants in the mansions along the Avenue occupied by the families of the men who owned the mills and controlled the banks.

Her brothers and sisters did not quite trust the Donegal outsider at first. They would have been happier had she met a nice Galway man, but Thomas was nothing if not persistent and eventually they came around. Two years and five months after their first dance, they married, and three months later the first Garrett to be born on American soil was on the way.

Declan Thomas Garrett was born at the stroke of noon on the first of May of 1924.

And Delia Mary Garrett died at two thirty in the afternoon that same day.

Being by himself was not a novel situation for Thomas, but he was never alone in raising the boy. Cousins on Delia's side were more like brothers and sisters, and Thomas had a brother out in the countryside, where Declan spent many a summer's day feeling like the city mouse among his country mouse cousins.

But Thomas was alone in his thoughts. Alone in his contemplation. He had grown accustomed to it but was never quite comfortable with it. He would smell her in the aisle at the A&P or hear her clear her throat in the pew behind him at mass. He saw her when he looked into Declan's amber eyes. He had known her for just a few of his fifty odd years, but she was part of his soul. Even though he still missed her every single day, he knew she was there. In the breeze. Somehow over his shoulder. And in Declan's eyes. That gave him comfort. Something to hold. It was simple, but it got him through.

Until now. This was different. This was fear of being by himself. He did not feel as alone when the gas clouds rolled over his head in the trenches. He did not feel this alone as he stood on the deck of the Baltic in the middle of the cold Atlantic, leaving family and every familiar thing in his life behind. He did not feel this alone when Dr. Felder wiped a tear from his blood shot eye and pronounced the only woman Thomas had ever loved dead.

***

Not more than a minute after he had set the newspaper aside, for the fourth day in a row, a young woman he had not seen before Monday turned the corner. She was early. For the past three afternoons, she had strolled by on the opposite side of the street, pushing a baby carriage that he knew had not come from Autenreith's Five and Ten down on the Avenue. She most certainly did not live on his street or any of the streets around the neighborhood. He knew this for two reasons. He knew every man, woman, and child within an eight block radius. It was his nature. And she wore bright print designer made dresses, hats and shoes that certainly were not bought on a mill worker's salary.

Each day, she glanced towards the house but made no eye contact with him and said nothing. Finally, on day three, Thomas had given her a nod and a wave. Day three also brought a return trip in the opposite direction, but she didn't look towards the house as she strolled by and around the corner. He thought it a bit peculiar, but he had other things on his mind.

As she passed, there was no eye contact and not even the slightest head turn. Perhaps the wave from the old man on the porch the previous day had been too forward, he thought. Off-putting in some way.

The awning between the porches flapped in the late summer breeze and he thought about what to do with the long day ahead.

"He-hello. Mr. Garrett?"

The shaky voice below his left shoulder startled him and he turned to see the elegant mystery woman standing on the sidewalk. She had appeared to be thirty years old from across the street, but upon close inspection she was much younger. He surmised twenty-two or twenty-three years old at best. No doubt the high-end dresses and hats helped to make her look more mature, but her face claimed otherwise.

He was a bit off-balance. She had addressed him by name, but he could not place her. Before he had a chance to respond, she continued.

"Have you heard anything? About Declan, I mean."

As he stood to face her, Thomas replied. "No. No dear. I haven't. You know my son, then?"

"Well. Yes. And I'm sorry for being so forward, but I heard you had received some word about him when I was in the market the other day. It was terrible of me to eavesdrop."

Thomas knew word would travel. Telling Agnes Larkin was as good as taking out a full page ad in the Sunday paper. The woman could not keep anything to herself if her life had depended on it. And Declan was a popular young man in the neighborhood. Well-mannered and handsome, he was the type that women loved, and men wanted to be around.

"No. I haven't heard anything more. I suppose it could take a while."

As he spoke, the gears turned, but he still could not place the pretty young woman.

"Forgive me dear. Do I know ye?"

Her voice quivered slightly as she answered.

"Oh no. Please forgive *me*. My name is Veronica. Veronica Sheldon."

"Well Miss Sheldon, it is a pleasure to meet you. I had never seen you on the street until the other day. How is it you know Declan?"

She smiled and said, "We met when he was working for the florist. He delivered flowers to my house."

She seemed to be comforted by the memory. Thomas appreciated the spark it sent through her. He also began to put some puzzle pieces together.

Declan had worked a couple of days a week during the school year and two busy summers for Gilman's Flower Shoppe on the Avenue. Every penny went straight into the bank towards tuition at the university. Sammy Gilman had sat behind Declan in just about every high school class and when he went off to college in New York, he had happily handed his sweeping and delivery duties to Declan. Mr. Gilman was secretly thrilled with the new boy, since, as he would often say, his Sammy had no interest in *earning* a paycheck, just receiving one.

Once a week for his entire tenure at Gilman's, Declan had passed through the ornate wrought iron gates onto the grounds of Willard Sheldon's mansion on Fifth Avenue to deliver flowers to the greenhouse keeper. For thirty odd years, Thomas Garrett had passed through the hulking gates of Sheldon Steel Company, doing his part to make that weekly delivery of exotic flowers possible.

"If you don't mind me asking, would it be Sheldon as in Sheldon Steel Company?"

Veronica's face reddened at the question. Thomas was not sure if it was anger, embarrassment, or a little of both.

"Well, yes. My grandfather was Marshall Sheldon." She looked away as if to spy something far down the block and her voice trailed as she continued. "My father is Willard Sheldon."

"Your grandfather, I knew him well. He was a good man."

She smiled as the words left his mouth. Thomas didn't have anything good to say about Veronica's father, so he said nothing.

"You're quite a way from that end of Fifth Avenue. It's a long walk."

"Well, I'm living in the carriage house behind my aunt's house on Tennyson Avenue. So, it is not far. It was empty, and I wanted us, Rose and me, to have a place of our own. Sometimes my father can be, well, difficult. And I thought it best."

Thomas gestured towards the back end of the baby carriage at the bottom of the steps.

"I see. Now may I assume this little one is Rose?"

"Yes."

As Veronica reached into the carriage, she asked, "May we join you on the porch?"

"Yes! Of course. Please, forgive me."

He opened the gate as Veronica lifted the baby out of the carriage. She was dressed in clothes as fine as her mother's. Veronica cradled Rose against her chest, carefully ascending the four steps to the porch.

As they reached the top step, she gently turned Rose towards Thomas and said "Mr. Garrett, this is Rose. Well, Rose Mary."

Thomas, by pure habit, reached out and Rose wrapped her tiny hand around his worn, calloused finger, smiling into his soul with her beautiful, familiar, amber eyes. For the second time in the short morning, he fought back tears, and he turned towards the screen door, trying to gather himself.

"Well then. Let's go inside. I'll put the kettle on."

The wooden screen door clacked against the frame behind the three of them and they disappeared into the house.

Just then the freckle-faced boy came rolling around the corner on that rickety bicycle like the wind.

Anywhere Else

Bob Simmons thought of all the places he would rather be in this moment. Digging his toes into the sand on the beach in Nags Head, beer in hand. Watching the Pirates beat the Orioles in game five of the 1979 World Series (*He would need a time machine or some sort of portal for that one but screw it. It's his daydream*). Strolling down the Champs-Élysées in Paris, France, towards the Louvre. Heck, he would take eating bar-b-que at a roadside shack in Paris, Texas, at this point.

Donna Haskins sat across the conference table from Bob. "Walter thinks he's funny. That's all. And he isn't. It's just mean. You need to do something about this!"

She was fed up. Just tired of Walter Slezinski (*misspelled Slezenski on his cubicle name plate, but he either had never noticed, or had never cared*) making her life at the law firm of Smith, Wombles, Rothchild, Carrington, Bainbridge, Krafft, Weatherby, Sumner and Gamble, P.C. (*Smith-Wombles for short*) a living hell. After twenty-seven years, she felt she deserved better than to have some Johnnie-Come-Lately abusing her good nature.

Walt Slezinski was a law-school drop-out and a legacy of sorts at the firm. His Uncle Thaddeus "Tadge" Nowicki, a brilliant legal mind, and heir to the world famous *Ace Packaging Peanut, Inc.* fortune, had been the first Catholic, and certainly first attorney of Polish descent hired at the firm. James Carrington III and James Sumner (*known around the firm as 'The Jimmies'*) had seen the value in hiring a young man who would walk through the door with all the contract and litigation work that goes along with having a veritable monopoly on the nationwide (heck, maybe worldwide even!) foam packing peanut market. And they had convinced the Board of Directors, in a lunch meeting in 1973 at the Duquesne Club, to look past his eastern European extraction and bring in the shining star of the University of Pittsburgh School of Law's class of 1974 as a law clerk.

It had not been without a fight, but Carrington III seemed to win over the room with his usual penchant for reason laced with humor when he summed up his plea by saying, "Gentlemen, it is a new day. He is as smart as a whip, he brings in a mountain of business, and it is not like we are asking you to hire an Eye-talian, or God forbid, a Mick!"

With that bit of bigoted whimsy, the room erupted in laughter (*except for the waitstaff and Wombles' driver, Patrick Joyce*), and the rest is history.

Tadge, over the next two decades, had led a successful effort to steer the firm away from hiring only, as his neighbor Tony Rebitini called them, "Pasty Anglos." Unfortunately, part of the more recent history stemming from that fateful day had come in the form of Walter Slezinski, paralegal, who had been hired at the request of Jeff Weston, Esquire, as a favor to his newly retired mentor, Tadge Nowicki, Of Counsel. It was the least he could do for Tadge, who had handed him a twenty-million dollar per-year book of business as he walked out the door.

Tadge had a soft spot for his baby sister Lynda, so when she had begged him to "see what he could do for Walter" down at the firm, he had asked Jeff to give Walt a shot as a paralegal. Tadge had no such soft spot for Walt, who had in his twenty six years put his mother through the wringer with bad decision after bad decision, despite having the same intellect as his uncle and some of the others in the family. In short, he had proven to be, in Tadge's words, "smart, but a lazy, pain in the ass." Walt had made it through a year and a half of law school at Duquesne University before crashing and burning, so he at least had some legal training.

He had been with the firm for half a year the first time Donna had complained to Human Resources about him.

Donna had been with the firm for nearly three decades. She had worked her way from file clerk to Assistant Director of Word Processing. From day one, she had always been a "go to" employee, volunteering to run the charity bake sale at Christmas, selling tickets to the firm Kennywood picnic every August (*One year, against Donna's advice, the firm sponsored a trip to a Pirates game instead of having the Kennywood picnic. As the kids say, Epic Fail! To her credit, she never gloated or said "I told you so" when the social committee met to begin planning for the next year's events*). She is the organizer of the monthly firm-sponsored happy hour for staff at the bar in the lobby of the building (*which, coincidentally, will take place just three hours after the latest meeting over her Walt problem*). Donna has always been a Smith-Wombles team player. Of course, she aspired to someday be Director of Word Processing. She was doing most of the work anyway, but she did not hold out much hope that Patty D. had any plans to retire soon. That was fine with Donna. Patty D. can have the glory. And the parking space. And the office. For now, anyway. Donna had always felt good about her efforts at the end of each day. Patty D. was nice enough, but she had never really gone out of her way for anybody (*Let's put it this way, she's no Patty J., that's for sure.*). If she were to drop dead or get hit by a bus, Donna would secretly be fine with that after whatever the appropriate period of mourning is for a just okay co-worker.

It would mean she'd get her own office, and she would get away from Walt. That would solve her current problem for sure.

Donna, along with being a team player, has always been one to keep up a tidy and cheerful workspace. If she has a flaw, it might be that her workspace is *TOO* cheerful. At any given time, her cubicle is adorned with no less than twenty, but no more than thirty inspirational, humorous, and even occasionally snarky wood block signs and wall hangings, along with rotating pictures of family events and trips to theme parks with those adorable nieces and nephews (*although, truth be told, Richie, Bev's second, is going through a gawky Goth phase, so he has been seen less and less in Donna's picture rotation over the past year*). Her décor is both seasonal and holiday based. But a few items, like her "First Coffee, then Talkie" wood block sign is on her ledge twelve months a year, right next to the "Be Kind" pencil holder.

And therein lies the rub.

Walter Slezinski is a passive-aggressive middle school boy in a grown man's body. And he has a disproportionate dislike for Donna's inspirational, humorous, and even occasionally snarky wood block signs and wall hangings.

He has not shown any feeling, one way or the other, towards her photographs thus far. Perhaps he has some standards. The jury is out.

When Bob Simmons had earned a master's degree in organizational management at Carnegie Mellon University, he thought his days of mediating squabbles between support staffers would soon be behind him. No more admonishing the mail room assistant for losing his temper with the UPS guy. No more handing out two-day suspensions to a court clerk *(and grandson of one of the founding members of the firm)* for getting a little too forward with the third-floor receptionist. He thought he had graduated to managing matters at the attorney level. Matching promising young associates with mid-level partners who need a capable and eager young mind to take their practice to the next level. That sort of thing. But it had not panned out that way. Consequently, he had found himself wanting to be anywhere else more and more when he was at work.

Bob had been waiting patiently for the firm higher-ups to see that he, and not Alfred "Woody" Woodworth, should be overseeing the high-level issues. But "Woody" was connected and not much older than Bob. In this way, he felt an unspoken kinship with Donna. "Woody" Woodworth was his Patty D. But he dare not articulate that aloud, given the current situation. He wouldn't want anyone to think he was biased.

That, and Bob was not much for small talk of any kind with the women at the firm, or anywhere else for that matter. Especially a woman he had admired, on many different levels, from afar of course, for the better part of two decades. He had never attended a firm happy hour. And it had been twelve years since he had last attempted the firm holiday party, getting to the restaurant, but never going in. This is not to say Bob had a reputation for being anti-social. Not at all. He makes a nice appearance. He signs all the get-well cards. He keeps up with elevator banter and water cooler talk. But he never shares *too* much. To some, he is an enigma. To others aloof. To others, just on the shy side. Still others assume the quiet, well-mannered H.R. Specialist just keeps his private life private, given the conservative nature of the firm. Despite his social trepidation, he was in his element at his job. And good at it.

He liked his job (*but if "Woody" went down in the same bus accident as Patty D., Bob wouldn't be too terribly upset*). He mostly liked his life. He was not much for change and was proud of the tiny two-bedroom house he owned (*outright*) in Oakland, just a few blocks from the much larger row house he had grown up in. Sure, he could have bought a house in another part of the city. Or even in the suburbs. After all, these days in Oakland he was surrounded by college students. But the commute was short. He was happy taking the bus in and out of town every day. And it was close to the Cathedral. He rarely deviated from the norm. He had always been a creature of habit. But with all his neat and tidy routines and uncomplicated ways, he still felt something was missing. He wasn't a loner. He didn't mind being alone. But he wouldn't mind being, well, *not* alone either.

Donna was hot under the collar, and this was the third meeting with Bob about Walter.

"So, what are you going to do about this, Bob?"

Bob had been looking past her out the window of the conference room, paying particular attention to the dancing fountain down in the square, wondering what the temperature was in Nags Head right then (*he wouldn't want her to think he was staring at the golden speckles in her almond shaped, greenish eyes*).

"BOB! ARE YOU EVEN HEARING ME?" Her voice was uncharacteristically loud. The change in tone had startled him.

"Yes. Yes. I hear you, Donna. I'm sorry."

Walter sat at the other end of the conference table, which could seat six comfortably. He chuckled at the exchange like a class clown.

Bob, keeping his desire to be anywhere else on the planet bottled up right next to his growing desire to pummel

Walter Slezinski, turned to him and said, "Look Walter, the first time you had the 'I'm with Stupid' sign pointed right towards Donna's cubicle. Then you sat in here and countered that complaint by saying Donna's '2 Blessed 2 B Stressed' sign should not be allowed under the firm's policy prohibiting anything religious in our workspaces. And she complied and removed it as a good faith gesture."

Donna folded her arms and sighed, as if reliving that defeat in her mind.

Bob continued. "Then, the second time we met, it was because some of Donna's favorite Disney nick-nacks had gone missing and were later found in the fourth-floor fridge."

Walt laughed and said, "Good thing you were able to solve that one, Bob. You're a regular Detective Lennie Briscoe."

Bob, still resisting the urge to get up and beat Walter to a pulp, continued.

"This time, you put a 'Who Farted?' wood block sign precariously close to Donna's ledge. That's just unacceptable!"

Walt snorted and said, "I'm not saying *she* farted! It's just a sign. Just some harmless humor, like all *her's*."

Bob glanced Donna's way and noticed tears had welled up in her eyes. It was not like her. She was no pushover. No shrinking violet. He had often observed her over the years at firm functions holding conversations with new lateral hires in the partner ranks as well as the newest secretaries. She worked hard to make the firm a welcoming place for everybody. He admired that. Her Smith-Wombles cubicle was her home away from home. She certainly didn't need Bob Simmons to fight her battles. She was more than capable. But like Bob, she had always been a rule-follower. She was willing to go through the correct channels and work with H.R. to resolve this problem. The tears in her eyes surprised him. She had moved past anger. She was hurt. Let down.

Walter did not seem to care about anything. That bothered Bob.

"No, it violates the firm policy on displaying anything in your workspace that could be deemed vulgar or distasteful by coworkers or visitors. You'll need to take it down immediately."

Walter nodded, as if to say he knew *that* was coming, and he'll be on Etsy in a few minutes ordering up the next batch of decorations that will lead to the next meeting. He had the attitude that he could sit through one of these meetings every month and there would be no real consequences.

And he was probably right. Despite his bad attitude and dislike for Donna's cheerful décor, he had proven to be a decent paralegal. The stakes were lower than being an attorney, but he was a better writer and more insightful than many of the firm's young associates. A classic underachiever.

But in this meeting, Bob had an Ace up his sleeve. Donna had no idea, and Walter certainly had no inkling of what was coming.

"Walt, it is not public, but I might as well let you know. Last night at the partners' meeting, Jeff Weston was voted in as a Class A shareholder. This means a bigger office for him on the ninth floor, 927, near the other partners in his practice group. But it also means since you work mostly on Jeff's cases, you will be moving upstairs with him."

Donna, arms still folded, let out an audible and exasperated breath. Bob knew she had to be thinking Walt was getting rewarded for his childish behavior. Sure, he'd be out of her hair, but he'd be upstairs in a bigger cubicle with the big shots. Some punishment that is.

Bob said, "You'll be in the available cubicle on the Third Avenue side, overlooking the parking garage."

Walt shrugged and chortled.

"Cool. Good for Jeff. Better view from up there, too."

Donna caught Bob's eye and smiled, and he knew it was not just because her nemesis was moving. That was a win, for sure. But she had also caught on to what had just transpired. She knew there were plenty of available cubicles on the ninth floor closer to Weston's new office.

But Bob was placing Walt next to Debbie Sanders. Thirty-three year Smith-Wombles veteran and secretary to Theodore "Ted" Wishart, Jr., the firm's managing partner. She is a Smith-Wombles team player, but in a different way than Bob and Donna. Deb is not a rule follower. She's a bulldog. No time for all that red tape. Her latest passion is axe throwing and legend has it, she was once a member of a fight club. If Walter steps out of line with Deb, she will manage it on her own terms, in a manner that is not outlined in the firm's policy manual. Sometimes there is blood. Not often, but occasionally. In some ways, she is a mystery and an enigma.

On Debbie's ledge sits a twenty-three year old photograph taken on the day of her daughter Emily's baptism. In the photograph, Deb is cradling "Baby Em," and her late husband Hank is to her left, smiling ear to ear. They are flanked by Emily's godparents, Hank's brother Ralph, and Deb's loyal friend and favorite coworker, Donna Haskins. The proud godmother had provided the "E is for Emily" frame.

Walt, none the wiser and happy to be moving upstairs with the big boys, filed out of the conference room first, eager to pack up his 'Who Farted?' sign and other belongings.

Bob sensed Donna wanted to give him a hug. A big, long, soft, and terrific smelling hug that he would have gladly accepted. But he could see that she had thought better of it, not wanting to break any rules. She exited, smiling, just before him.

Then she stopped on a dime, turned back to him and said, "Hey Bob, I'll see you at happy hour tonight, right? I owe you a drink."

He nodded, and managed to spill out, "Oh, yeah. Sure. I'll be there."

As Donna walked back towards her home away from home, Bob stared out again at the dancing fountains, and at that moment, for the first time in a long while, he had stopped wishing he was anywhere else on the planet.

Home

We reached the third day of our journey and, to be honest, things were not going well. Actually, that's not entirely true. Just the three days since we arrived in the States were rough. This has been a much longer journey. Getting from Europe to New York in a tin can stuffed with six thousand grimy, eager soldiers and sailors was a piece of cake compared to our cab catching fire in Manhattan, the broken-down passenger train somewhere in Jersey, and two flat tires on the rickety bus between Philly and Pittsburgh. Even though it seemed like the gods had conspired against me, I was happy to be back on friendly soil after a couple of years of mostly hell on earth.

By the time the bus pulled up to the station, darkness had given way to the light of the new day. The avenue was empty except for a delivery man tossing bundles of newspapers onto the sidewalk from the back of his truck. There were no cabs at the bus station, and it was just as well. I could walk the last couple of miles. At least my fate would be in my own hands, and a little bit of solitude would be fine with me. I could not remember the last time I had been alone for more than three minutes.

As I made my way towards Oakland, the sun nudged higher and Forbes Avenue slowly came to life, people emerging from their homes. Most of them waving or giving me a "welcome home soldier" as they went about their morning routine.

A woman in a housecoat stopped sweeping the stoop and steadied herself on the wooden broom stick as I approached. I nodded and smiled, adjusting the duffle bag from one shoulder to the other as I passed. She tried to muster a return smile, but a tear trickled down her weathered cheek and she looked away. From the corner of my eye, I caught the gold star flag in the window of her immaculate row house.

My old man used to say if the guy on the next barstool is going on and on about all the glorious things he did in the war, then he was never really at war.

I adjusted the duffle again, my thoughts going back over there, knowing I'd never be able to undo any of it. A steady flow of letters from home kept me going. My brother Joe told me about a couple of guys who went overseas as smart and stable as they come and came back soft in the head. Real top of the class types. FUBAR.

To my right, the mills on both sides of the Monongahela sputtered flames and smoke into the morning air as I walked up the hill, around the bend into Oakland. Another thing the old man used to say is the smoke and the smell of the mill put food on the table and a roof over our heads.

I figured a bunch of men from the neighborhood died, but Joey spared me from too much of that. I guess he didn't want to add to the pile. He's smart like that. Spending months getting to know a man to the point where you can smell his mother's goddamn cooking, then watching him bleed to death, isn't something I'll be bragging about at Coyne's Tavern, that's for sure.

The duffle bag felt a little bit lighter as I hit the crest of the hill and turned down Kraft towards the Boulevard. The home stretch.

Tony Russo was good at knocking all that horrible mess out of his head. At least it seemed that way. He was funny, smart, and looked all of about fourteen years old. Tony swore he was nineteen, but nobody believed him. Every Italian kid I knew started shaving in the fifth grade. I don't think Russo ever had a razor in his hand. All he wanted was to get home for Sunday dinner. Tony said his mother had fed practically the whole damn block every Sunday. I think that's why we got along. He was a Brooklyn kid straight out of central casting. When he talked about his neighborhood, he could have just as easily been talking about South Oakland. I knew a lot of guys like Russo, but at the same time, he was one in a million.

One freezing cold night, right before going into the forest, as we sat up against a couple of boulders at the base of a hillside trying to get some sleep, he said, "I'd rather be a bird than a fish."

I turned to face him. "What the hell are you talking about?"

"My ma used to tell me and my sister this story. Something about a fish who wanted to be a bird. The fish was mad because he was a fish and all he could do was swim around in a pond. But if he were a bird, he could fly anywhere he wanted to go all day long."

He turned towards me, leaning on his elbow. A sliver of moonlight found its way through the clouds and bounced off Russo's face. "It's like that around here, you know. Some of us are destined to be fish, and some of us get to be birds. You know what's crazy, Sully? For the life of me, I can't remember if that fish became a bird at the end, or if he just stayed in the muddy pond forever."

That was it. Neither of us said another word. I didn't get much sleep that night, but he slept like a baby.

The next morning, we trudged into the freezing cold forest and Russo was one of the first soldiers hit. Square in the chest. I dragged him behind a tree and kept us both covered for as long as I could. He quivered on the cold and rocky ground, leaves and dirt sticking to the blood as it rolled out of the gaping hole. His eyes were wide open, but it was like he was looking through me. He clutched my forearm tight, and with his last breath said, "Keep being a bird, Sully."

As I turned onto Juliet Street, I shifted the bag and thought again about the worn down gold star mother with the broom watching guys like me walk down the street, and Tony's mother looking at an empty dinner plate for an eternity of Sundays.

By the looks of it, even though the world was vastly different, nothing much had changed on the block. My pace quickened with each step as I drew closer to the red brick house with the green and white awning shading the same chairs and same glider situated in the same spots on the porch. I stood on the sidewalk and studied the house. My house.

The wind changed direction just enough for the smoky odor of the mill over the hill to give way to the fresh, familiar scent I had been dreaming about every day and night for months. It was unmistakable. I dropped the bag on the stoop and walked between the houses towards the backyard.

I paused and stood silently at the gate, taking it in. The smell. The warmth of the morning breeze. The barking of a faraway dog. In that moment, it was as if little else existed and nothing else mattered. I watched her dance gracefully between the billowing sheets in an elegant ballet, moving around the wicker laundry basket. I pulled up the latch on the gate, interrupting the serenity with the harsh screech of metal against metal. Unfazed, she clipped the last clothespin to the line and turned slowly towards me. She smiled the same soft, sweet smile from our wedding picture, as a tear rolled over her freckled, sun-kissed cheek.

I was home. Tony was right. I'd rather be a bird than a fish.

Reno

Teddy watched Pete take off the beat up old bowling shoes and put them in the blue leather bag, one on each side of the brand new monogrammed ball, and said, "Why do you keep those worn out shoes, Petey? There's nothing left of them. They just got those brand new black leather Brunswicks in. Eight bucks a pair."

Pete zipped up the bag and sat up. "Well, for one thing, I'm a lefty, and my shoes are lefty. They only have righties. Lefties are special order. Second, these were my old man's shoes. I guess it's just hard to part with them."

"Fair enough," said Teddy. "But you can keep those and order new ones. Reno just ordered lefties for Leonard Harris from Frazier Street, and they came in two weeks. Put those in your trophy case or on your mantle."

"Alright, wise guy. I'll think about it."

They gathered their bags and started towards the lockers. Teddy nodded at the man behind the counter to their left. "See you next week, Reno."

Pete followed suit. "Okay, Reno. Take it easy, buddy."

Reno looked up from the cash register and waved. "See ya fellas." He generally didn't have a lot to say.

As Pete and Teddy wound their way down the fluorescent-lit stairwell, Teddy said, "So, Reno, he's your neighbor, huh?"

"Yeah, well, he was when I lived with my mum. Second floor of the duplex next door. Said he used to be an accountant or bookkeeper or something before moving here."

"He looks more like he'd push a broom than a pencil," Teddy said. "What's he doing working at the bowling alley?"

The dings and clicks of the pinball machines and the sounds of rolling bowling balls conquering pins faded, and a cool autumn air hit them as they spilled out onto Forbes Avenue and went left towards Atwood Street.

"The glamour and excitement maybe?" Pete said. "Seriously, one time he told me he knows all about the stock market and bonds and all that and invests his bowling alley money. He said someday when he has enough, he'll just drop everything and go live on a beach somewhere."

As they crossed Forbes Avenue at Atwood Street, Teddy said, "It's like he just showed up behind that counter one day. Nobody knew who he was or anything. He was just there."

"Well, he just showed up in the duplex the same way. Maybe five years ago. He's not from around here. He told me he is from out around Chicago or something."

Pete blew some warm air into his hand and said, "I asked him a couple of times where he came from, and he just says, 'here and there' all vague like. Not exactly mysterious, but not eager to talk about himself either."

"Don't you think that's a little, I don't know, off or somethin'?" asked Teddy.

"Well, he's a decent guy. No trouble. Works two jobs. My mother says she sees him at church at the Cathedral and his downstairs neighbor Alice Perkins says he volunteers down at the soup kitchen a couple times a month. I think he just keeps to himself is all."

Teddy nodded towards the newspaper stand in front of the drug store. "Happy says he has never seen anyone as lucky as Reno when it comes to gambling, so he ain't a complete choir boy, Petey."

Anthony "Happy" Lorenzo owned and operated the newspaper stand at Forbes and Atwood. If you wanted a paper from the old country, Happy would get it delivered to you from Krakow or Rome or Dublin. If you wanted a New York Times, or a local paper from the armpit of America, he'd get that for you, too. More importantly, if you wanted to place a bet on a horse or play the numbers, Happy was the man to see. If it was happening in Oakland and Happy didn't know about it, then *nobody* would have known about it. Or it wasn't really happening.

Pete said "I know he ain't a saint, Ted. But I'm saying he seems like a decent man, is all. For a fella that doesn't talk a lot about his past, I mean he doesn't show any signs of being a louse, you know?"

Teddy shrugged and said, "I get it, Petey."

He swung open the door to the Oakland Café and a rush of warm air and the smell of neighborhood bar greeted them. The place was nearly empty with just a few other bowlers and a couple of regulars dotting the booths and the bar. They took a seat in a booth along the wall and a framed, signed photo of Pie Traynor stared down at them.

Teddy gestured towards the bar and said, "Hey Johnnie, two Irons and a couple bags of pretzels, over here."

From behind the bar, Johnnie shot Ted an exasperated look over the wire rims of his glasses and said, "Come and get 'em, Teddy, tonight's my night off from waiting tables."

Pete hopped up, grabbed the beers and pretzels from the bar and as he sat back down, Teddy said, "What's been eating at you kid? Your average is fifteen pins down this year, and it can't just be those broken down old shoes."

"I don't know. Nothing really. I guess I just got some things on my mind. I don't know."

Teddy took a long drink of ice-cold Iron City, looked at Pete for a few seconds and said, "Bull shit, Petey. I know you too well. Nothing phases you, not since we were kids."

"I just got some stuff on my mind is all. I worry, like anyone else."

"What are you worried about, Petey?"

"Well, my mother. That asshole she's married to. I think he hits her. She denies it, but she has had a couple of black eyes. She tries to cover them up with makeup, but I can tell. And the other day I saw a bruise on her arm, up near her shoulder."

"Holy shit, Petey, what are you going to do about it?"

"I don't know. I asked her about the bruise on her arm right in front of him, and she got all nervous and said she bumped it. I gave him a look and he wouldn't make eye contact, but I could tell he was real mad. I don't want to say anything else because that might make it worse for her. But I swear to God I'll beat his ass if I see another mark on her."

"Damn, Pete. Everyone knows that family is nothing but trouble from way back. Gangsters and thugs. They're in deep. For every decent Quenten there are ten bad ones."

Pete said, "I guess she thought she got the good one. Listen Ted, I tried to reason with her, but there was no talking her out of it. Horatio is a charming bastard for sure. And she was lonely. It was just me and her, no other family, and I have my own life now."

Teddy opened his bag of pretzels and let Pete keep talking.

"I'm no dummy, my own father was no prince. He came back from the war, I don't know, different. He had a mean streak when he drank, and I wouldn't be surprised if he didn't backhand her once or twice. I was a little kid, but I remember hiding under the dining room table a few times. But he was mine, you know what I mean? Warts and all."

A rush of sirens and blinking lights whooshed against the glass block windows of the bar and down Forbes Avenue as Teddy spoke.

"I don't know what to say, Pete. I thought maybe they were talking about lay-offs again down J&L or you were having girl trouble or something. I didn't know you had that going on. To be honest, I kind of disagree. I think you need to do something about it."

The sirens faded to a far-away whisper as Pete answered. "Like what, Teddy? I don't want to get my mother in any more hot water with this guy."

Teddy shook his head as if to say he didn't have an answer, but someone needed to stop Horatio Quenten.

"I don't know Ted. It's a tough one. Let's just drop it for now. I don't know what I'm gonna do about it, but maybe you're right. I can't let it go."

They veered away from the subject at hand, made some small talk for a few minutes, and ordered another round.

The door to the Café swung open abruptly and the handle bounced against the wall.

"Pete! Petey Thorpe? You in here?"

Officer Shaw darkened most of the doorway as he peered around the bar, allowing his eyes to adjust to the dimly lit room.

"Right here, Mr. Shaw, right here!" Pete stood and took a step towards the broad shouldered cop.

"Grab your jacket, son, and come with me."

***

Bewildered, Pete sat in the back of Shaw's police car as it sped down Meyran Avenue towards a wall of blinking lights and commotion. As they approached his mother's house, Pete began to expect the worst. If only he had taken things into his own hands. If he had been more direct, maybe this wouldn't have happened.

Shaw stopped the police cruiser in the middle of the street. No need to pull in. As Pete exited the back of the vehicle, a detective approached, and waving a fat pencil Pete's way, asked Shaw "Is this the son?"

Shaw shook his head and replied, "Yes, the son has a name. It is Peter."

"What's going on? Where's my mother?"

Pete attempted to get past the detective, who grabbed him by the arm as another uniformed officer stepped in his path.

"Whoa, whoa. Hold on, fella. You can't go in there. Cool it."

Pete stopped long enough for the detective to take the wind out of his sails. "I'm Detective Joseph. Take a deep breath. Your mother is not in there."

"What? Where is she?"

"We don't know where she is, but she is not in there. The only thing we know for sure is there is a dead man in the kitchen. One Horatio Quenten. Her husband, no?"

Seeing Pete's stunned confusion, the detective continued. "The man in there is dead from a single gunshot wound to the head. Right between the eyes, as a matter of fact."

Detective Joseph followed Pete's face closely, looking for a tell or some sort of hint of anything. Nothing.

"I don't understand. Where is she? She must be somewhere. Maybe she is at the store, or church."

"No stores or churches open this time of night, son. All we know is she isn't here. We aren't saying anything one way or another, because, well, we really don't know yet what the hell happened or where she could be. But if you know anything, it will help."

"If I know anything? Five minutes ago, I was having a beer, shooting the breeze at the Café. Now I'm here. I'd say Quenten probably has some enemies and one of them took care of business, that's what I think. And either they have my mother, or she is going to come home to this!"

"Doesn't sound like you like Mr. Quenten very much, Peter."

"You could say that, Detective. I'm not a fan of the fellow. He was a mean cuss, and not too nice to my mother sometimes. So no, I don't like him at all."

"I get it kid. I've had plenty of run-ins with that clan myself. Do you know anyone in particular that might have a beef with Horatio Quenten?"

"What? No. Jesus Christ! Just about everybody. Where could she be? Whoever did this could have hurt her too!"

"Calm down, son. We have plenty of people out looking for her, and looking for whoever did this to Mr. Popularity in there."

Detective Joseph ushered Pete to the curb and sat him down.

"Listen son, go home and get some rest. There is nothing you can do here."

"I have to be here when she comes home! I can't go nowhere!"

Joseph nodded and attempted to put Pete at ease.

"We'll be here for a good long time, and then we will have a patrol car out front. If she comes home, you'll be the first one we notify."

As the words left his mouth, Detective Joseph did not have one ounce of hope that he would ever see Pete's mother again. Usually in these matters it is the spouse or significant other. Almost every time. But that wasn't his hunch in this case given Horatio's long list of enemies. The type of enemies who would have no trouble putting a bullet in his head. Her pocketbook and forty dollars were untouched on the dresser in the bedroom. There were small signs of a struggle in the kitchen. A broken coffee mug. A few drops of blood here and there. He figured Horatio did some other gangster wrong and paid for it and the woman was just collateral damage. An unfortunate casualty. But he wasn't about to share his unproven theory with a shook up young man.

"And don't go out there looking for her. Go home so we know where to find you should we need you. Understand?" He turned away from Pete and walked back into the house, leading the county coroner to the kitchen.

As if out of thin air, Reno appeared at the curb. "What the hell is going on?"

Pete, as best he could, brought Reno up to speed.

Reno, hands on hips, shook his head and said, "Holy shit, Pete! Holy shit! I told her that son of a gun was no good! Don't worry, Pete. I'm sure she's safe. We'll find her. Don't you worry."

Until that moment, Pete had no idea Reno and his mother had ever spoken beyond a polite 'hello.'

***

Months passed. No leads. No news. Pete checked in daily first with Detective Joseph, then at some point with the missing persons bureau after Detective Joseph had handed the case over. Nothing. Reno, despite his claims on the night of the murder, didn't seem to be making any attempts to find Pete's mother. Pete chalked it up to Reno just trying to make him feel better.

Pete had no close relatives. His mother had no real friends. He had turned over every stone and exhausted every avenue and had come up empty. He held out faint hope she was out there somewhere. He was surprised nobody from the Quenten family had come around looking for answers. For the most part, he had resigned himself to the idea that whatever thug put a bullet in Horatio's skull had done the same to her but disposed of her body somewhere else for God knows what reason. He couldn't sleep. He wasn't eating much. And he had become all but nonexistent around the neighborhood. He hadn't been bowling since the incident and nobody could blame him. Everybody was fine with it. He'd come back when he was ready. How do you make small talk with a guy going through all of this?

Teddy had been giving him space but made sure to check in on him every so often. Same with Reno, although there was a distance to Reno that had not been there before. Pete could not quite put his finger on it, but Reno didn't seem to be too concerned about any of it.

Finally, on a breezy summer evening, Teddy stopped by Pete's and said, "Let's go. We're going around the corner to Isaly's for a skyscraper cone. Maricopa, like when we were kids. I'm buying."

Pete had been looking for an excuse to get out, knowing at some point he would have to start doing more than sleeping, working, and worrying. And ice cream was probably better than going to the Café and drinking, so he obliged.

"Alright, Teddy, you got me. I'm in."

"Atta boy, Petey!"

By some small miracle, they had beaten the evening rush at the ice cream store and filed through the line. A cheerful, freckle-faced kid served up two Maricopa skyscraper cones and they made their way out onto Forbes Avenue and started to stroll down the street.

"Man, I love this ice cream, Teddy."

"There's nothing like it. If I had to pick, I'd say it's my favorite, although chocolate chip isn't bad. Listen to us, like a couple of little kids."

They laughed at their childlike enthusiasm for a simple ice cream cone, then walked for nearly a block in silence.

"So, Pete, what's the latest? Anything?"

"Nothing. I check with the police all the time. No leads, no nothing. I'll be honest, Ted. I think I'm getting a little better about it. A little bit. But for a few weeks, I didn't know if I was going to make it. I'm still a mess. Don't get me wrong. I mean, she's all I have. I know I got friends and all, but we've been through everything together, me and my mum. But I'm saying I don't think it'll kill me, too, ya know?"

"I can't even begin to imagine, Petey. Not for a minute. But yeah, you got friends, and we're practically like family, right? I know it ain't the same, but..."

"Yeah, I know that Ted, but the worst is I get nightmares, like of someone killing her all over again, and I can't help her. Ever. It's terrible. Then in the back of my mind I know someday I'll have to figure out what to do with the house, look into what little money she had. All that dismal stuff."

They found themselves directly across from the Strand Lanes as Teddy finished off his cone and said, "What do you say, Pete? Let's go get an alley and bowl a few frames."

To Ted's surprise, Pete said, "Yeah sure, why not?"

They crossed Forbes and as they ascended the steps to the bowling lanes their trained ears could tell there would be no trouble getting a lane, even though they hadn't called ahead. Unlike the wall of sound of constant rolling bowling balls, falling pins and the machinations of automatic setters during the league season, they heard the noise of maybe three active lanes.

"Well, look what the cat dragged in." Dane Lally peered over a pair of crooked readers at Pete and Ted, as he folded a newspaper over and set it aside.

"You working the evening shift, Dane? What gives?"

"Well, we're hiring if you're looking for something more exciting than whatever it is you do down the City-County Building. What is it anyway?"

Teddy chuckled and said, "Marriage licenses, Dane-o. Something you seem to be allergic to so far, old man."

"I just ain't met the right girl yet, Ted. Still holding out. You boys want a lane, or are you gonna throw all your spare change in the pinball machine like when you were kids?"

"Ha. No, we'll take a lane, Dane."

Pete looked around and said, "Hey Dane, where's Reno?"

"That's why we're hiring, Petey. Reno comes to me a couple of weeks back right after all the leagues finished up and says he finally has enough saved up enough to take his riches and move, I don't know, down south or out west, I guess. He didn't say where."

"Holy moly! Come to think of it, I haven't seen him in a couple of weeks. Since Memorial Day. He didn't say a word to me!" Pete was staggered by the news. He thought Reno would have at least said goodbye to him, given the circumstances.

"I don't know, kid. You know Reno. He was never much for details. He was a, you know, what do you call it? An enigma. Worked here for all that time and never told me too much about himself, and never once missed a shift. And his register was never off in spite of the fact that I know he'd let people slide if they was having a tough go of it, ya know. My cousin Mario down on Meyran said Reno was looking for work. If he was an oddball or crooked, I figured Mario would have known. Or someone else would have told me. So, I hired him, and he worked out just right.

Stand-up guy. I paid him straight cash, so I didn't care where he came from or where he was going."

Pete said, "Yeah, he invested all that money."

"Right. Smart fella. Reliable. I ain't gonna find another Reno, that's for sure. Take lane three, fellas. Just got oiled up. Oh, and Petey, you owe for your locker. I haven't seen you since, well, you know. So, you can pay me whenever."

"Oh, yeah, no problem. Sorry about that, Dane. I'll settle up tonight."

As they sat down and the lights to lane three flickered and came on, Ted said, "What do you make of Reno just taking a powder like that, Petey?"

"Well, he always said when he had enough money, he was gone. I guess he figured out he had enough and that was that. It's a little weird that he didn't say goodbye, Ted. But it's also Reno being Reno, I guess."

***

Summer rolled on and Pete slowly returned to doing all the things he had enjoyed doing before his life had been turned upside down. Taking in the occasional Pirates game at Forbes Field. Double features at the Schenley Show. Pick up softball games at the Oval.

Things were still strange, and he knew they would never be the same, but he also knew he had to keep moving and at least attempt to live his life. He had stopped avoiding people as interest in his mother's case seemed to wane from constant well-meaning and the occasional not so well-meaning questions to some whispering and nodding in his general direction. He had no problem with that. He could handle it.

One breezy summer afternoon in one such attempt to get back to his normal routines, he stopped at the bakery on Forbes for a loaf of bread and a couple of brownies. He made a bit of strained and somewhat confusing conversation with the pretty young Italian woman behind the counter, who smiled politely at him as she handed him his change. As the bell on the door clanged as it closed behind him, he turned right towards Atwood confident that his two years of Italian at Schenley High School was finally paying off.

As he reached the corner of Atwood, Happy Lorenzo called to him from the newsstand.

"Petey, where have you been? I haven't seen you all week."

"Oh hey, Mr. Lorenzo. How are you doing?"

"Not bad Pete. Hey, Bob Friend pitched a gem yesterday, huh?"

"Yeah, looks like he's a bright spot anyway. Him and Frankie Thomas. He hit another dinger yesterday."

"I'm just hoping they don't lose a hundred this year. Gotta have hope for the future I suppose."

"Maybe so, Mr. Lorenzo. Seems hard to do that when they can't seem to get it together, ya know."

As Pete drew closer to the newsstand, Happy reached under his counter and said, "Oh hey, by the way, that news you wanted is here."

"What do you mean? I didn't ask for any paper?"

"Sure, kid. You have been looking for some news. I got it for you."

Happy pulled a folded newspaper from under the counter and handed it to Pete. "Here it is. There's a special insert in there. Don't drop it. I also circled an ad in there you're gonna want to read."

Pete unfolded the newspaper to reveal the masthead. *Reno Evening Gazette. August 8, 1955.* A small lime green envelope peeked out of the top of the newspaper.

"Like I said, Petey. It's that news you've been looking for. Don't lose that insert. That's the important part."

Happy stuck his head out of the newsstand and looked both ways.

"That ain't no souvenir. Get me? Read it and get rid of it."

Pete, until that last comment, had not been following Lorenzo's line of conversation.

"Um, sure thing Mr. Lorenzo. Thank you."

Pete held the newspaper tight in his left hand, making sure the envelope did not see the light of day, nor move from inside the paper. He hurried back to the Oakwood Apartments and made his way up the flight of steep stairs to Number 25.

He opened the door and dropped the bakery bag on the counter to his left and sat down in the wingback chair, nearly knocking over the lamp.

He fumbled to open the envelope, which contained one small piece of matching paper, folded in half. He unfolded the page, revealing a short note, written in his mother's unmistakable and impeccable handwriting.

Safe and well. More when we meet again.

His heart nearly thumped out of his chest and his hands shook. She was alive.

In reaction to Mr. Lorenzo's cryptic message, he then turned to the classified ads in the newspaper. Happy had circled a three line ad in the real estate column in red ink.

Lovely three bedroom bungalow.

Private Beach and Fishing Dock

North End, Casey Key, Osprey Florida

A classified advertisement for Florida real estate in a Reno, Nevada newspaper. He sat back in the chair and let the relief wash over him. She was alive.

He committed the note and real estate ad to memory, got the Zippo lighter from the kitchen drawer and burned the paper, note and envelope, washing the ashes down the drain.

He didn't know when and he didn't know how, but he would make his way to Osprey, Florida at some point very soon. For the time being he would be happy just in the knowledge that she was alive and safe.

With the weight of the world lifted from his shoulders, he walked around the corner and down the block to the newsstand. He slid a brownie across the ledge and said, "Thanks for the, uh, news, Mr. Lorenzo."

Looking up from his change drawer, Happy winked at him and asked, "What news, Petey?"

Pete laughed and nodded, knowing they would never speak of it again. As Petey turned to walk away, Happy chuckled and muttered to nobody in particular, "That Reno. Full of surprises."

Movie Star Parking at the White Tower

Christmas, 1966

3Pop turned off Meyran Avenue onto Euler Way and brought the crowded Dodge to a slow crawl as it neared Atwood Street. Snow flurries fell to the windshield and met their immediate demise as they hit the warmth of the car.

"Movie Star parking. Six years running," he said.

Pop was proud of his secret Christmas Eve parking spot in the alley alongside the White Tower. The fact is nobody was out on what was now technically Christmas morning. 1:47 a.m. to be exact.

"I thought he'd never stop talking. With his holier than thou attitude and Boston accent," he said.

His wife peered around Kathleen, who was wedged between them in the front seat, and said, "Joe, it's a sin to talk about the bishop like that, especially just after mass."

"Come on now, Fran, you know it's true. It's like he's always looking for someone to kiss his ring."

Her credo was if she didn't have something good to say, she didn't say anything, but he knew her silence and ever-so-slight nod was an admission of agreement.

Matty, seated directly behind his father in the back seat between Mary Alice and the door, hitched forward.

"So, what's movie star parking?" he asked.

Pop said, "So let's say there's a movie premiere, Matt, and Steve McQueen rolls up in his limo. He gets to park right in front of the theater, because he's a movie star."

The Old Man was more than happy to explain his concept to the youngest of the McCann brood as it was a new term to Matty, but as evidenced by the near synchronized eye rolling of the girls, it was old hat to the rest of the family.

"Oh, I see. Well, we're in an alley next to a hamburger joint, so maybe this is more like Channel 2 weatherman parking," Matty said.

The entire car, including the old man, erupted with laughter. Sometimes it was hard to believe he had just turned eight years old.

Their mother shook her head and said, "Matty and Martin, run in with your father to help carry the burgers."

A little over ten years separated Martin, the oldest, and Matthew. Kathleen, Mary Alice, and Annie came one after the other between the boys. Despite the age difference and positions on opposite ends of the birth order, the boys had a solid appreciation and understanding of each other. For Marty, Matt was part brother, part mascot. In return, Matty was all too eager to play that role as long as he was occasionally asked to tag along to a Pirates game with Martin and his friends, or a pick-up basketball game at the Y on Forbes Avenue at the top of Coltart Avenue.

Even though they were a decade apart, they were known in the family as "the twins." The resemblance was uncanny, and hardly anybody outside the family could differentiate between Martin's first grade school picture and Matthew's. It didn't hurt that they were both wearing a blue dress shirt and the very same red tie (Matty's stroke of genius), or that the folks down at the "Classic Touch School Photography Company" hadn't bothered to change backgrounds in fifteen years.

Martin and Matty spilled out of either side of the back seat while Pop hopped out of the driver's seat and said, "I'll leave it running. Shouldn't be long. The place looks almost empty."

As if cosmically drawn to it, "the twins" found themselves directly under the light of the streetlamp, knowing their mom and the girls would be watching. The old man shook his head and continued into the White Tower as Matty ducked behind the building just down Atwood beyond the streetlamp and Martin struck a perfect Ed Sullivan pose. Snowflakes fluttered through their makeshift spotlight as he rocked and swung his arm towards "offstage left" and Matty appeared as if acknowledging the introduction and applause and launched into a mime routine that went from juggling, to plate spinning, to tap dancing and ended with the star on one knee, hands in the air, blowing kisses to the "crowd" as Ed Sullivan doubled over in laughter a few feet away. The boys could hear the muffled laughs of Mom, Mary Alice, and Annie from the car, and could see Kathleen, stoic as ever, trying not to break from the middle of the front seat. Success.

The old man emerged from the White Tower with three sacks of burgers, and waving one towards Martin, said, "Thanks for the help, pal. Hop in before you get arrested for loiterin'."

As the smell of burgers permeated the warm car, the annual edict came from the front passenger seat. "Don't open those bags until we get home and into the kitchen! I mean it, Marty!"

As the Dodge turned onto Meyran Avenue from Fifth, Kathleen turned, winked at Matty and said, "Hey kid, your plate spinning was good. But you'll never get out of the alley with that act."

The car again filled with laughter as they rolled down Meyran Avenue.

Kathleen continued. "Singing is what's going to get you on Sullivan. Sing it for us, Matty. You know the one."

Matthew smiled, turned towards the window as if concentrating on the snow covered cars and launched into a soft and near-perfect a cappella Little Drummer Boy. His young voice filled the car, taking the family with him to a hopeful and happy Christmas.

***

Christmas, 1967

"How can this be happening? This can't be real!"

Mary Alice wiped tears from her puffy cheeks as they walked by the nurses' station. A big boned woman in an immaculate white uniform and pillbox hat fiddled with the dial of a transistor radio, settling on "the sounds of the season on KQV."

The three sisters stood, shaky and bewildered, at the end of the shiny, dark hallway on the fifth floor of the Children's Hospital, looking down on Fifth Avenue.

"Father Baker is in there praying over Matty like it's going to do any good." Annie, too numb to be angry or sad, shook her head as she spoke.

Mary Alice said, "He's just in there going through the paces until the funeral director gets here. Father Baker seems like a fine man, but I doubt he has any conviction about one word coming out of his mouth right now. But he knows it's important to Mom."

Kathleen had always been the most devout of the three, but that had changed recently.

"What kind of a god takes two sons from a mother in the span of three months?" she asked. "Baker couldn't even look us in the eyes when that other pompous windbag was in there yesterday assuring mother that 'God has a plan.' What might that plan be? How do you look a woman in the eye and say that, knowing her eldest came home in a wooden box after three months in Vietnam, and her baby lies on his deathbed, hit by a car?"

To ease the tension, Annie said, "Look down there."

She pointed towards the intersection of Atwood Street and Fifth Avenue below and said, "You can see White Tower from here. Remember last year Marty and Matty under that lamp, doing the Ed Sullivan thing? Seems like forever ago."

Kathleen watched from afar as the flurries danced through the light of the same streetlamp as a year ago. She closed her eyes and engulfed herself in that memory.

"Matty, on the way home, singing like an angel…"

As the last word fell off her tongue, she was reduced to a heap of uncontrollable sobs, Mary Alice and Annie not far behind.

As she gathered herself enough to speak, Kathleen said, "He was an angel. An angel on earth, that boy. And Marty. We couldn't have asked for a better set of bookends."

***

December 1989

Gracie McCann stood outside The Decade at "The Corner of Rock-n-Roll," or the corner of Atwood and Sennott to the uninformed, and watched the snowflakes dance sideways in the air above her as she waited.

As he approached, she smiled and could feel a few butterflies in her belly. She had to admit she had never really had that sort of reaction to a guy before. Usually, in her limited experience, after four dates, she has been ready to move on. But there seemed to be something different about this one.

For one thing, they had met in a computer lab and not in a bar or at a fraternity party. He was smart and interesting. It didn't hurt that he was nice looking and polite. For some reason, she had no problem letting down her guard with him. That was new to her.

He was head over heels. Yes, they had just met, but he had secretly had his eye on her since the third week of the semester. It seemed he would see her everywhere. The football game, the record store, in line for the Rocky Horror Picture Show. Gracie was also somewhat of a regular at the computer lab where he spent ten hours a week working in return for a modest reduction in tuition. Each time he saw her, he had assumed she had no idea they were on the same planet, let alone within a few feet of one another. And each time he had vowed that next time he would speak to the auburn haired mystery girl. And each time he had caught a glimpse of her almond shaped green-brown eyes, he had lost his nerve.

Until one fateful day in the computer lab, something had given Nick DePietro the courage. Well, not quite. Truth be told, it was Gracie who had initiated first contact.

"Hey, uh, Nicholas Nickleby?"

She stood peering down at him from the opposite side of the counter. He looked up and was startled as he came eye to eye with the mystery girl.

"I'm sorry, what was that?"

She gestured towards the book, entitled 'The Charles Dickens Companion,' that was cast aside on his desk.

"Your book. I called you Nicholas Nickleby. A little Dickensian humor. Very little, I guess. Anyway, the printer's out of paper."

"Oh." *He nodded and chuckled nervously.* "It's for a British Lit class. And you're half right, anyway."

"What do you mean?"

"On my name. You're half right."

"Your last name is Nickleby? Wow. What are the odds?"

He let out a laugh and shook his head. "No, the other part."

"I know. I couldn't resist. Well, Nicholas, whatever the other half is, the printer?"

"Oh right. Sorry." *He was struggling for words but glad to be talking to his mystery girl.*

He pulled a ream of paper from under the desk and came around the counter and stopped in front of her.

"DePietro," He said.

"What's that?"

"That's the rest," he said. "My Name. Nicholas DePietro."

"Oh. Got it." She held out her hand and said, "Well, Nicholas DePietro, I'm Gracie. Grace McCann."

"Well Grace, it is nice to meet you."

He shook her hand as if they were making a business deal, held on a second or two too long, and afterwards stood motionless in front of her, lost in those green-brown eyes.

"Likewise, Nickleby." She said as she motioned towards the printer. "But that printer isn't gonna fill itself."

That interaction led to a coffee date, which led to a movie date, which led to a pizza and a movie date.

And here they were on a weeknight about to embark on their first bar date to see a live band.

As he crossed Sennott Street and moved towards her he said, "It's coming down a little harder now. I didn't think it was supposed to snow."

They greeted each other with a hug that was less awkward than she had expected. She laughed and said, "I'm a little surprised I got you out on a school night."

Noting her sarcasm, he said, "Yeah, my mom even lets me walk home from school by myself sometimes."

As they approached the door to The Decade, he held the door for her, and she smiled like a cat that ate the canary.

"What?" he asked.

"Nothing. I just had a little flashback."

Her grandmother always told her to *'find yourself a door holder.'* When Gracie would ask her what that meant, she would say *'You'll know it when you know it.'*

Nick shrugged it off and asked, "So who is this band, anyway?"

"Miracle Legion. They're from Connecticut. They play them on WPTS a lot. They're *so* good."

Nick paid the cover charge for both. The door man greeted Gracie by name and gave her a hug. He examined Nick from head to toe before smiling and giving him a friendly albeit forceful slap on the shoulder.

As they walked through the bar, Gracie said, "That's just Timmy, he grew up a couple of houses down from my grandparents. I have about a hundred unofficial big brothers in this neighborhood."

They made their way into the next room and found a spot along the wall near the soundboard beneath a mostly legible copper sign that listed all the rock and roll legends who had played at the club.

Gracie ordered a couple of draft beers from the back bar and returned just as the band took the stage, which was on the opposite side of the room and was dark except for some Christmas lights strung through a wreath on the back wall. No introduction. Just a spotlight on the lead singer, who stood with his head cocked to the side.

The usual barroom chatter dimmed to a low buzz as the drummer began a "rat a tat tat" on the snare and the singer rocked slightly on his back foot. Then he sang.

"Come they told me, pa rum pum pum pum..."

What followed was a beautiful and faithful Little Drummer Boy that achieved something rare from a rock and roll crowd. Silence. In this wonderful, odd, and mesmerizing moment, Nick glanced at Gracie, and she had tears streaming down her rosy, freckled cheeks.

He leaned in and whispered, "Are you okay?"

She tried to answer, but the tears turned to sobs, and she hurried past him and out the side door onto Sennott Street.

He followed as the rush of cold air greeted them and she leaned against the dark wood of the building, directly under one of the recessed lights on the overhang. The spotlight draped her as if she was in a one woman play as she tried to gather herself.

Nick placed a gentle hand on her back and asked, "Grace, are you alright? What was that?"

Finally composed enough to speak, she said, "Come with me."

"What? We just got here. You like these guys. That was awesome. Don't you want to see them?"

"Timmy will let us back in. We're only going up the block."

She turned right onto Atwood Street towards Forbes Avenue. The snow was steady and sticking to the pavement as they crossed the street and up the hill towards Fifth Avenue.

She crossed Atwood in the middle of the block, and he dutifully followed her fresh footprints.

She stopped under the streetlamp at Atwood and Euler Way and tried to count the snowflakes as they dropped through the light onto her face. White Tower was long gone and had been replaced by a mundane shop on the back end of a bland, brown rectangle of a building.

"What are you doing, Gracie?" Nick asked.

She said, "Well, I'm going to tell you why I lost it back there. I promise it makes sense."

He shook his head, marveled at her as the snow seemed to fall around her and not on her and said, "Okay. Let's hear it."

She proceeded, in faithful detail based on various versions of the story she had cobbled together over time, to recount the highs and lows of the last twenty-two odd years and what had led her to the spot under that streetlamp at that very moment.

She began her tale in 1966 on that final night of Movie Star Parking at the White Tower and smiled when she got to the part about Matthew singing Little Drummer Boy.

She told Nick, "I have never once in my entire life witnessed my mother listen to that song the whole way through without crying. Sometimes it is just a little, sometimes it is like me at The Decade tonight. It never hit me like that before. I guess I was thinking about her."

She moved through time as if she had been there for every moment. "My Uncle Marty's draft number came up and he went straight from basic training to Vietnam. He was only over there for a couple of months when he was killed somewhere in a jungle."

She sensed Nick's shock and shook her head.

"It gets worse. Not too long after Uncle Marty died, my Uncle Matthew was hit by a car on a snowy night like tonight, and he died too. Just like that, in a matter of months, they were both gone."

"Oh my God, Gracie! That must have been awful for your mom, not to mention her parents."

"Yeah. It's a little weird calling them my uncles because I never met them. That, and Matty was just a little boy. But everyone always called them my Uncle Marty and Uncle Matty, kind of like they were still there."

She spun and stuck out her tongue to catch the snowflakes like a child.

"My Grandma wrote Marty a letter every week. The last two letters were sent back to her, unopened after he died. She still hasn't opened them and says she doesn't even remember what she had written. She told me once the only thing in the entire horrible mess that she has been thankful for was that Marty never had to endure sleepless nights in that hell on earth after Matty died."

Nick was content with listening and watching Gracie as she talked and moved under the streetlight, making deliberate footprints in the fresh snow. There was gravity and sadness to her story, but she seemed to have an uncanny ability to keep that in a separate compartment from her compulsion to live in the moment. He had never met anyone like her.

"I can't even imagine it," he said. "Two sons in three months. How do you even deal with that?"

Gracie stopped, one foot in front of the other, arms straight out, as if balancing on a tightrope.

"I have wondered that my whole life," She said. "I guess they just dealt with things in their own way. My Aunt Mary Alice was the strongest. Apparently, that was a surprise. Aunt Annie somehow muddled through, and although she did, let's just say she 'experienced' the sixties pretty hard and spent the seventies recovering from that."

And Kathleen, by her own accord, had also rebelled, giving her already grieving and reeling parents more to worry about.

"Mom says she fell in with the wrong crowd. But my Aunt Mary Alice says it was more like my mom was the leader of the wrong crowd," Gracie said.

"She met a guy who was a few years older and got, as the old folks say, 'in trouble' about a year after Matty died."

Nick asked, "What do you mean 'in trouble?'"

Surprised Nick didn't understand the euphemism, Gracie smiled, cocked her head to one side and said, "uh, in the 'family way?' Pregnant. Knocked up. In biblical terms, 'great with child.' Jeez, try and keep up, Nickleby!"

Nick laughed and nodded. "Oh, ok. Sorry Grace, I'm twenty-one, not eighty. Sorry I don't speak 'Old Timer.' Go on."

"Anyway, the man disappeared into the ether. Left town. She felt like she was on an island in her own home. Scared. Angry."

Gracie wiped snow from Nick's shoulder and continued.

"I guess Gram was just trying to keep what felt like the final thread from unraveling, but she never really told her what to do. Grandma told her she'd know in her heart what was right. That's it. She speaks in riddles sometimes, my Gram."

Gracie, for the first time, stopped moving and looked Nick in the eyes. "I don't know if she ever, you know, considered anything else, but here I am. She has always said even if she had to go it alone, she knew she would figure out a way to make it work."

Nick said, "My Nonnie, my grandmother, says when God takes something, he gives you something in return."

Gracie took Nick's hands in hers and said, "Wow! That's the first thing my grandmother said to my mother when I was born. Oh man! Do you believe that?"

"Yeah, I mean, the universe or God, or whatever you believe. Somehow there must be some balance to the whole thing, right?"

Gracie smiled deep into Nick's eyes, but the happiness left her face as quickly as it had appeared, and she continued.

"My Pop. My grandfather. He fell off the wagon. Big time. He had stopped drinking when Martin was born, but losing his sons was just too much for him, I guess. And by the time he had climbed back on the wagon, when I was like eight or nine, he was tired, sick, and just needed a place to rest."

The grandfather Gracie McCann knew was far different than the smiling man carrying sacks of burgers out of White Tower.

"Funny thing, he was never mean. Never, well, nice either. He was just sort of vacant. Gone. He died when I was ten. The first person I ever knew who had died."

She looked over Nick's shoulder at nothing in particular. "Sometimes I'd pull these old photo albums out from under my grandma's bed, and we'd go through them like they were story books. I guess in a way they were. My favorite, though, was watching home movies with her and my mom. The best ones were from right before Matty and Marty died. It took Gram a long time before she could watch them. But one day, it was like she was just ready to do it."

Nick brushed snow from her shoulder, and they ducked under an awning.

"She would point out everyone in the movies. Laugh. Cry. Laugh. Cry. Smiling at her sons as if they were in the room. I remember one time we were watching one that they filmed of the little league parade right down there on Forbes. Pop was walking by smiling and waving. We were sitting tight on the couch, and I looked up at her. She was looking at Pop like she was seeing him for the very first time."

Gracie again cocked her head to the side and studied Nick, as if she was trying to memorize him.

"The Pop in those home movies and in those photo albums, with the pompadour and glint in his eye, that's the man I always remember. Even though I never really knew him."

She recalled to Nick those first few years living in the old neighborhood with her mother, aunts, and grandparents.

"My mom was young, working her butt off. It was somber. Sad. Though not all the time. Mostly when I was really young. But I never felt unloved or unsafe."

She reached out and again took Nick's cold hands into her own.

"My Grandma still calls me 'Princess Grace' and sometimes calls me 'Saving Grace' because she says I showed up when they needed me most."

She had left no stone unturned, telling Nick the happy things, the sad things, and the things, up to that night, she had never shared with any person outside her family. But for some reason, she had no problem sharing with Nick.

Somewhere in the story between her mother being escorted home at age seventeen in the back of Officer Campbell's police wagon, and Aunt Annie coming out at Thanksgiving dinner, Nick looked deep into Grace's sparkling eyes and thanked his lucky stars that the printer had been out of paper.

***

December 2004

The auditorium under Sacred Heart Church was crowded with moms, dads, grandparents, a couple of great-grandparents, a few favorite aunts and uncles, and countless unruly siblings. All of whom had thus far been subjected to an hour and a half of Christmas carols sung, in a manner of speaking, by over a hundred students from Sacred Heart Elementary School's grades Kindergarten through two.

Miss Murphy, in her first year as second grade teacher in room 103, had been hoodwinked into putting together the annual Early Elementary Christmas concert. Her enthusiasm was unwavering, and to be honest, not many parents were sad to see Mrs. Stewart pass the baton. It had been long overdue. But if they had one complaint about Miss Murphy's inaugural production, it was the length. She sensed the restlessness in the crowd and made a mental note to keep it under an hour for the spring show. But she also knew she had an ace in the hole. A big finish.

As Sister Barbara Ann ushered twelve of her top kindergarteners off the stage, Miss Murphy thanked everyone for their patience and attention, asked for one last round of applause for the kids and all their hard work, and waited for the young boy in the perfectly pressed blue dress shirt and red tie to take his place in the middle of the stage.

As the boy situated himself, she said, "I think you will really enjoy our final number. We have Matthew Martin DePietro singing an old favorite."

The boy nodded at Miss Murphy, turned to the audience, adjusted the microphone like an old pro, looked out into the general direction of his family, and said, "This is for anyone who is a fan of Movie Star Parking at the White Tower."

He then launched into a near-perfect a cappella Little Drummer Boy.

In the third row, Kathleen smiled and made a futile attempt to fight off the tears as her grandson commanded the stage. She clutched the weathered and perfectly manicured hand of her mother as Gracie, with little Maria on her lap, and Nick, with baby Joseph in his, beamed at their eldest.

His young voice filled the auditorium, taking the family and everyone else along with him to a hopeful and happy Christmas.

There Was This Guy Across the Street

There was this guy across the street. In the second floor apartment. Right across from my grandparents' house, which is right next door to my family's house. He was a nut. Totally bonkers. He would stand in the window in his birthday suit for hours at a time. Naked as a jaybird. Like a mannequin. He looked like Charles Manson, but like I said, totally naked. Charles Mannequin. That's what we called him on account of him looking like Manson and standing so still in the window. We didn't want to make too big a deal of it because he had a few screws loose.

On the one hand, he wasn't hurting anyone. But on the other hand, little kids, and a lot of females, from college girls all the way to old ladies on their way to and from the A & P at the top of the street walk up and down the block. I'm thirteen, so technically I'm a kid too, but growing up in this neighborhood, you see all sorts of crazy things. So, to be honest, a naked hippie standing in a window like a statue isn't too high on the list of nutty things I've seen.

But we get people from all over the place parking around here visiting one of the hospitals or the museum. My old man says all those people looking for parking spaces fled for the suburbs so their kids wouldn't have to put up with things like naked hippies in windows or the smell of weed coming from the apartment building next door.

We have cousins who visit from the country, way out in Cambria County, but they visit us enough to see their share of crazy things. Plus, believe me when I tell you, there is a lot of off the wall stuff happening out in the country where they live. Their neighbor is just about the prettiest girl I've ever seen, but she chews tobacco. Red Man. Like a relief pitcher for the Pirates or something. And she drives a tractor. Not for work, but just to get from one place to another, the way I ride my ten-speed.

Anyway, back to the naked guy across the street. We had theories. My old man figured Charles Mannequin was feeling the aftereffects of Vietnam. He said he served in World War 2 with some guys who were never the same afterwards. Guys who had seen a lot of action. He was lucky. He hadn't seen too much of that. At least not enough to make him go over the deep end and stand around naked or anything.

Our next door neighbor, Mrs. Kelly, said she saw a show on channel 13 about LSD, and she swore Charles was on an acid trip, or had done too many acid trips and his brain was fried. Mrs. Kelly always went in for the most extreme theories on everything, but nobody counted her out on this one. It wasn't too off the wall.

Either way, once we were laughing at Charles and my mother got plenty mad at us. Looking back, she was right. As usual.

So, one of my cousins, Sally, was visiting Grandma for a few days. Like I said, we live right next door in an attached row house. Me and Sally were born three months apart, right after JFK took office. Anyway, if we had it our way, we would have been sitting on the porch all day waiting for Charles Mannequin to flinch. But Grandma wasn't having it. She didn't want us, especially Sally, due to her being a girl, sitting out on the porch staring at a naked man in a window. She said we shouldn't be looking at another human being as if he was a circus act or a zoo animal. She said he was clearly suffering, and we should never forget that every person has dignity. No matter what. And we should offer up some prayers for him instead of sitting there gawking. I can't blame Grandma. She was right. But we weren't doing it to catch a glimpse of his private parts or to make fun of him, we were doing it to see if he moved a muscle. He had the uncanny ability to stand there perfectly still for minutes at a time. The longest he had ever gone was nine minutes and thirty six seconds. We timed him. We had a stopwatch and everything. We also tried to stand still for that long. It is harder than it looks.

Before Grandma put an end to our surveillance mission, we had the brilliant idea to act like we were reading the newspaper, except we put little holes in the paper so we could see right through and up to the window. We didn't know if Charles Mannequin even knew we were watching, but we didn't want to take any chances.

Since Grandma didn't want us spying on Charles, we were packing it in for the day when it all happened. One police car came up the street, and the other came down. Not fast with sirens blaring or anything. They were creeping along real slow. They stopped in front of the house, and two cops got out of each car, and they all looked up at Charles Mannequin in the window. They muttered some stuff to each other, shook their heads, and probably wished it was their day off. Three of them moved towards the front door of his house and one of them turned towards Sally, Grandma, and me.

Charles didn't move anything below the neck. But he looked down at the officers on the street as if he had no idea what all the fuss was about.

The officer who came towards us didn't look too much older than me and Sally. It was a combination of him being young and looking even younger. I had never seen him around Oakland, so I figured he had to be a rookie. We knew all the cops from the Number Four Police Station and all the University of Pittsburgh cops. Being on their good side always seemed like a good idea. It had paid off a couple of times for my older brothers when they got in some hot water. So anyway, that's probably why the other three sent him over to talk to us instead of going in to tend to the naked guy in the window. I bet they figured approaching a naked hippie takes more experience than approaching a friendly looking old lady in a housecoat.

So, Grandma tells the Rookie all about the young fella in the window, as she calls him. Like how we didn't want to make too big a deal about things because we could all tell he was having some sort of mental problem. Or else he wouldn't be standing in a window naked, looking like he hadn't been to the barber in a couple of years. Sure, she told the Rookie he was making things uncomfortable by being naked in the window, but he wasn't hurting anyone, and sometimes you must give people a little bit of grace when they're suffering. The Rookie agreed with her on that one. She also told the Rookie that the young fella in the window has been living there for about three months and that occasionally a woman comes to visit him. A sister. That's what Grandma said to the Rookie. She reached into the pocket of her housecoat and handed the Rookie a small slip of paper. A sister. That one was news to me. But I didn't doubt it because my grandmother never missed a trick. And what she didn't see, Mrs. Kelly saw, and they compared notes at least once a day.

It turned out, according to the Rookie, a nurse from the hospital had been the one who called the cops. She wasn't mad or anything, but she told them every day when she would walk by on the way to her shift, there was a naked man in the window. She was concerned for his safety. You can't blame her. What she didn't know was that my grandmother, Mrs. Kelly, and my mother were all keeping an eye on Charles Mannequin too. That didn't come out right, but you know what I mean. They were looking out for his well-being. If things had ever taken a turn, like if he did anything creepy, or maybe come out onto the street in the buff, they would have called the police too. To be honest, I couldn't believe this was the first police visit in three months. We've had plenty of neighbors who are very well-known to every cop in the Number Four Station.

The Rookie thanked Grandma, nodded at me and Sally, and went over to join the party in Charles Mannequin's apartment. By this time, Charles was away from the window, and we couldn't see what was happening. Maybe twenty minutes later, the lady my grandmother was talking about pulled up in a brand new Dodge. The sister. She looked totally normal. Really put together. Like she worked downtown in an office, or maybe in one of the hospitals in a desk job. I was surprised because she didn't look like the kind of lady who would have a scruffy hippie that stands around naked in windows for a brother.

After maybe fifteen more minutes, the police officers all emerged from the house and the Rookie waved at us as all four cops got in their cruisers and drove off. The sister and Charles Mannequin were not far behind. He was dressed in jeans and a black and white flannel shirt. Which, come to think of it, were the same clothes he was wearing the two other times I had seen him with clothes on, outside of his apartment.

The sister looked at Grandma and gave her a tearful smile and a wave as she helped Charles into the passenger seat of her new Dodge. It was a familiar smile, not like one you'd give a total stranger. As if she had known all along that Grandma and her crew were looking out for her brother.

And just like that. No more naked hippie in the window. That was the last time Charles Mannequin was ever in the apartment. The sister came around one last time and packed up his things. He didn't have much.

A week or two later, the apartment was rented to a mouthy couple who played their music too loud and liked to smoke reefer on the porch roof. Grandma said she liked the naked hippie better. He was less trouble.

Fast forward a couple of months. Early one Sunday morning Sally and I were walking down Fifth Avenue near Frick School and there they were, right across the street. Strolling along, smiling, and not really saying anything, but they were happy. That was clear. We didn't recognize him at first because, well for one thing, he had clothes on. Blue jeans, a new red and blue plaid flannel, and an army jacket. Maybe my dad was right. He was also clean shaven and had been to a barber. He still looked like he would be afraid of his own shadow, but he looked ten times better than he did when he was naked in the window. The dead giveaway was the sister. I recognized her immediately, because she looked even more put together in her Sunday best. At first glance they still looked like they didn't exactly belong together. But if you studied them for a minute, the laughing and smiling told a different story. We were glad.

We couldn't wait to tell Grandma.

Home Court

Spring, 1986

I am not good at losing things that have been a part of me.

On a long weekend home from school, I hop in the old man's beat-up '77 Volare and make my way to the Boundary Street Playground down the hollow. Panther Hollow.

Overcast. Seventy-five degrees. A great day for some hoops.

I pull in, grab the basketball, and as I get out of the car I hear, well, I hear nothing.

No dribbling. No trash talk. No start and stop of rubber soles against the blacktop.

I enter the playground and flag down a kid popping wheelies on the asphalt court.

"Hey, where'd the hoops go?"

He looks at the place where the pole, backboard, and basket used to be, circles around me on the bike and shrugs his shoulders.

"They took 'em out 'cause too many college kids were coming down and starting trouble."

His abbreviated story leans a little to one side. I had been on the court for a few dust ups that had been equal parts naïve college bravado and native Oakland swagger.

Shock. Sadness. I stand on the court taking it in, dribbling, aware of the slight slope (a home-court advantage).

The place looks different. I feel different. Mixed memories.

The only time I had ever dunked a basketball was on this court. Downhill, with a half-deflated ball on a rim that was a good three inches shy of ten feet. But it still felt good.

Once I watched a mouthy college kid get his leg busted with a baseball bat wielded by an angry and fearless Oakland lifer. We had tried to warn the kid.

I grew up on this court.

Birds chirping. A waterfall flowing off the cliff on the other side of the train tracks. Cracked asphalt. Broken chain link fence. The harsh echo of the bouncing ball.

I am lost. Angry.

The kid on the bike comes back into the playground riding side saddle.

"Hey mister, the hoops ain't gonna grow out of the cement. They're gone."

Mister? What am I, sixty? I'm twenty-one.

"Yeah. I know, kid. And don't call me mister."

He nods, and glides away down Boundary Street, butt high off the seat, balancing himself on the pedals.

I pull up my dribble. The world, at least my piece of it, stands still.

One last look around. I get in the car and drive away.

I guess this is what people mean when they say you can't go home again.

Phenom

The boy sat on the bleachers watching the man on the riding mower cut the infield grass. Large trees beyond the left field foul pole blocked the morning sun, creating shadows over much of the ballfield.

A grass infield. How about that, the boy thought. He had never seen a grass infield on such a small baseball field. Let alone one that was in such good condition. Like a big league ballpark, just smaller.

Advertisements hung on the outfield fence for "Honest" Bob Tate Chevrolet, Laurel Point Savings Bank, Johnson-Whaley Funeral Directors, Lally's Insurance, Laurel Point Drive-In ("Just a mile out of town on the Bypass!"), and Kwik-Towne Supermarket. Just over the left centerfield fence was a large, dark green scoreboard with white letters and numbers. To the left of the scoreboard was one final ad for Smitty's Bakery with a large, iced, sprinkled, donut in the middle. Below the donut in bright, pink letters, batters were invited to "Hit it in the hole and get a free Baker's Dozen!"

Fat chance of that happening, the boy thought. The hole was maybe big enough for a volleyball. A pretty small target from 215 feet away.

A flagpole stood high just beyond the scoreboard. The boy noticed the Stars and Stripes flapping ever so gently towards right field, although he felt no breeze at ground level.

Along the fences down the first and third base lines hung red, white, and blue bunting, which reminded the boy of pictures he had seen in books of old World Series games.

The dugouts were enclosed with cinder blocks on three sides, painted dark green and covered with slanted, tin roofs.

Behind the backstop was a small building, also made up of cinder blocks and painted to match the dugouts. He wasn't sure, but this looked to the boy like a snack stand he had seen once at a minor league game.

The most impressive thing to the boy were the lights. Six high wooden poles, each topped with two rows of four lights strategically surrounding the field. Night games for little kids! How about that, he thought. He had watched two innings of a night game three days earlier from way beyond the left field fence before making his way out of town down the Bypass road.

The man, by this time, had finished cutting the infield and had switched to the outfield grass. He had a system, and he knew down to the minute how long it would take to cut the entire field and the grassy areas in foul territory.

He had noticed the boy sitting on the top row of the wooden bleachers. It struck him as odd for two reasons. The boy did not look familiar at all. It was also not lost on the man that the boy did not seem eager to leave. The boy, the man thought, was not just passing time watching some fellow ride a mower around a ballfield. The boy had a purpose.

The man liked to get the grass cut early while the shade trees were still providing cover from the sun. Once he got rolling, he did not like to take breaks. He liked to keep to his system. But curiosity was getting the best of him. Who is this boy? Why is he sitting alone at the ballpark just watching?

Once he had completed the infield, outfield, and the grassy areas in foul territory, the man drove the mower through a gate on the right field side and backed it up a short ramp into a wooden shed that had been painted the same dark green as the dugouts and snack stand.

The man emerged from the shed, removed his ball cap, wiped his brow with the back of his hand, and closed and padlocked the door.

Just as the man expected, the boy had not moved from his spot at the top of the bleachers and made no effort to leave as the man made his way across the infield.

As the man walked through the gate next to the dugout, he said, "Morning, young man."

"Good morning, sir," the boy said.

"Sir? At ease, soldier. Around here most folks just call me Coach Mac, or plain old Coach."

"Well, uh, good morning, Coach Mac."

Coach Mac, the boy thought, looked like he had been a ballplayer at one time. Tall and rangy, but not skinny by any means. Strong. And he had a farmer's tan.

"I haven't seen you before, son. What's your name?"

"C.J., sir... er, I mean Coach Mac."

Coach Mac stood at the bottom of the bleachers, hands on hips, studying his new acquaintance.

"Pleased to meet you, C.J. To what do we owe the pleasure of your presence at the Laurel Point ballfield this fine morning?"

The boy chuckled at Coach Mac's old timey question and said, "I was wondering if it's too late to, um, join the league."

Coach Mac cocked his head and said, "Like I said, I've never seen you around before. Do you live here?"

"Uh, well, I just got here the other day. From Pittsburgh," the boy said.

"You just move here?"

"Um, yeah."

"Well usually it would be too late to join the league, being as the season's more than half over, but a couple of teams have had a whole lot of bad luck with injuries and vacations and such."

The boy smiled at the thought of getting on that field.

Coach Mac took a minute and then asked, "You any good? I mean have you played much baseball?"

"Yeah. Um, yes. I played for a couple of years in the little league back home. I do alright."

Coach Mac started towards the dugout and gestured to C.J.

"Come on kid, let's see what you got."

He made his way to the refreshment stand building, fiddled with a jangly bunch of keys attached to his belt, and unlocked the door. He returned a few seconds later with a couple of baseball gloves, a bucket of balls, and a bat.

As he tossed a well-used glove to the boy, he said, "I hope you're a righty."

"Yes, uh, throw right, bat left. Well, I can kinda switch hit, but I'm better from the left."

He said it in a matter of fact manner, which made Coach Mac chuckle.

"Oh, well then. Go out to shortstop, I'll hit you some grounders."

Mac started easy. Hitting slow grounders, all of which the boy fielded cleanly, with perfect footwork and mechanics. The boy, knees bent, swayed and shifted his feet, popping his fist into the mitt in anticipation of the next grounder. Every return throw to Mac started with a crow hop and ended with the ball landing a foot or two away from the bucket.

"Nice work, C.J. Is short your usual position?" Mac asked.

"Usually second base, because our shortstop was really good. I like to pitch, and I like centerfield, too." The boy stood, glove hand on his hip and continued, "I guess I'll play anywhere. I just like to play."

Coach Mac decided to ramp it up a bit, putting a little more on the grounders. The boy continued to field them seemingly without effort.

As Mac laced a hard grounder towards the hole between short and third, he asked, "So who's your favorite baseball player?"

The boy backhanded the ball on the third bounce and before tossing it back to Coach Mac, said, "It's a tie between Maz and Clemente. Mazeroski because he can turn two better than anybody. And Clemente because, well, he can do everything."

"Good picks. Both great players."

"Yeah. I mean yes. Our little league field, where I used to play, is right next to Forbes Field. Right behind the outfield wall. So that is pretty neat, but it isn't nice like this field. I mean we don't even have grass on most of the outfield, let alone on the infield like this. This is the nicest field I've ever seen."

Coach Mac took a second or two to survey the field and said, "Thanks. We do our best to keep it up. It's a little extra spiffed up for the All-Star game on the Fourth of July, well, the third."

Mac had the boy move to the outfield and the results were the same. He awaited each swing, weight on his back foot, like a soldier in the contrapposto position, then watching the ball at the crack of the bat, he adjusted. Perfect mechanics and instincts on every fly ball. Every throw home bounced once or twice and landed within three feet of the bucket.

Batting practice was no surprise to Coach Mac. The boy had a quick, compact swing and made solid contact with every decent pitch, lacing line drives into the outfield, and hit two fly balls within a couple of feet of the right field fence. No jittering, no wasted movement with the bat. He laid off the few bad pitches and missed none of the good ones. Mac had him switch to the other side and the results were still good but not great.

C.J., thought Coach Mac, is a mere mortal when he bats right handed.

"Let me see you pitch a few," Mac said.

He trotted off the mound and grabbed a catcher's mitt from the bag and took the position behind home plate. The boy took the mound and proceeded to throw smoking fastballs with pinpoint accuracy wherever Mac positioned the mitt. Inside corner, outside corner, a little up in the zone, straight down the middle. It didn't matter. Out of twelve pitches, Mac only had to move the mitt twice. Barely.

Once Mac had seen enough, he walked towards the du
on the third base side and motioned for the boy to
him. They sat side by side on the bench looking out at
pristine field, taking in the perfect summer morning.

Coach Mac said, "Well, you know how to play. That's
sure. Where'd you say you played?"

"Oakland. In Pittsburgh, right near Forbes Field."

Coach Mac wanted to ask what prompted a move from
city to a small town, but he didn't want to be too forw
with the boy.

"Right, right. Okay, here's the deal. My team, the Orio
we're, well, we're hurtin' for certain. Three kids w
broken arms, out for the season, including my best t
pitchers. One kid shows up maybe half the time. T
leaves me with ten total, well, nine and a half."

The boy smiled and looked up at Coach Mac and said, "
are you saying I can play for your team, Coach?"

"Well, here's what happens next. Your dad or mom
going to have to come down to the field with you to fill
the sign up form. And we're going to need a bir
certificate or Baptismal certificate. Something to pro
your date of birth."

The boy looked sheepishly out towards the pitcher's mound and said, "Well, I have a birth certificate, but I can't get my mom or dad to come here to sign me up."

"What do you mean, son?"

"Well, it's a long story, but I am not living with my parents. My dad died not too long ago and my mother, well, she has troubles. Like with her nerves. So, she is in a hospital in Pittsburgh."

"I'm sure sorry to hear that, son. So then..."

"My uh, grandparents' house is off of the Bypass road. Past the drive-in, almost to the airport. I'm staying out there."

"Okay, then one of them is going to have to come down to the ballfield here and sign you up. We have a game Thursday night at 7:00. Can you be here at 6:15?"

"Sure Coach. Um, can you give me the sign up form so we can fill it out and then bring it back when we come on Thursday?"

"No problem. Let me get one for you from the soda-pop stand."

***

For the boy, the clock ticked slowly between that day and Thursday. For Mac, it was like any other two days, with the

added task of notifying the other seven managers of his new player. Most were fine about it, given Mac's predicament with filling out the line-up card. A couple of the more competitive guys, like Jerry Reefman, from the first place Cubs, and Chet Kingman from the last place Red Sox, were leery.

"So, you want us to just let you sign up a ringer at this point in the season?" Jerry had asked.

"He's no ringer, Jer. If I would have gone over to Davisburg and poached him from Bob Winston's team, you'd have a point. But this kid, he just moved here, showed up at the field, and he wants to play. Sounds like he's had a rough go of it lately, too."

Well, maybe he isn't a ringer, Jer-Bear, but he sure as heck can play, and you can bet your hefty butt I ain't gonna tell you that, thought Mac.

Jerry grumbled a little more, but ultimately had given in.

Poor Chet had been saddled with the youngest and least talented team in the league. He had figured maybe playing nine against eight against a short-staffed Orioles squad might be his best shot at a win. But after a meek protest, he relented and didn't want to be the only guy standing in the way of a young boy playing organized baseball.

The boy showed up a few minutes early, birth certificate and form in hand, ready to play some ball. He made his way to the first base dugout, where Coach Mac had a neatly folded cream-colored button down uniform with black and orange trim on the bench. He patted the uniform with his hand and looked beyond the boy.

"Is anyone with you, C.J.?"

The boy shrugged and said, "They can't come today. They're not in very good shape."

He handed Mac the birth certificate and sign-up form and waited for a response, hoping this would not be a deal breaker.

Mac checked out the application and certificate, buying himself a moment. League rules state a team can start a game with eight players but can't go with seven.

"Well, listen, C.J., the form is in order, and the birth certificate is good, but I'm really not supposed to let you play without meeting a parent or guardian."

Dejected, the boy said, "I know, Coach. But all I want to do is play ball."

"Okay. Listen, here's the deal. If one of your grandparents can't make it to the next game, I'll stop by and say hello. Introduce myself."

"Does that mean I can play today?"

Coach Mac smiled and said, "Yeah, you can play. Shoot, I will only have eight today *with* you, so without you we would have to forfeit. Go change in the equipment shed."

With that, the boy scooped up the uniform and bolted for the shed. He emerged a few minutes later wearing the uniform and a grin that a sandblaster would not have been able to remove from his face.

"Looking good, my man! Let me see your stirrups," said Coach Mac.

The boy stopped and held up a foot, looking down at the black baseball stirrups.

"Smaller loop in front, higher loop in back, right Coach?"

"Right. Where'd you learn that?" Mac asked.

"My coach in Oakland taught us. Wear your stirrups wrong, run a lap."

"Pretty impressive, C.J. Most kids don't know how to wear their stirrups right."

As the boy placed his neatly folded street clothes on the bench he said, "Coach, can I use that glove I used the other day? I don't have one with me."

"Sure thing. Just keep it with you until you get one."

By the time Coach Mac returned with the glove, some of the other players had arrived and were milling about the dugout, looking at the new kid as if he had three heads.

Mac tossed the glove to the boy and said, "Boys, take a seat on the bench. C.J. stand up here with me."

As the boy stood, Mac's first base coach and assistant manager down at the Kwik-Towne Supermarket, Willis Stewart, entered the dugout.

"Howdy Coach Will. Just in time. Coach Will, fellas, this here is C.J. He is now a member of the Orioles."

The boy nodded at the bench and said, "Hey. Hi."

Coach Mac went down the line and each player introduced himself. The boy could feel them sizing him up. Trying to figure out what the new kid was all about. Where does he live? Why doesn't he go to our school? Why is he just coming around in July?

Coach Mac tapped the eraser end of his pencil against the scorebook and said, "We have the Cardinals today. You know what that means. They'll throw Covetti for the first three, then Smitty for the last three. So, let's jump on Covetti. Green light all the way. If it's close, swing away unless it's three and oh."

The boy knew this meant Smitty was the stronger pitcher of the two.

"Okay. Signals are the same as always. Belt is take. Right forearm is swing away. Left forearm is bunt. Brim of the cap is steal. C.J., the second signal I give is the one that matters. Do you know what that means?"

The boy nodded and said, "Yes Coach. First sign is a decoy, right?"

Coach Mac was not surprised that he knew this.

"Yes sir. Alright, here's the lineup. Lincoln Meyers, second base. Jake Sewell, right centerfield. Billy Jenkins, third base. Rudy Meyers, clean up and on the mound. Bobby Rich, shortstop. Freddy McGee, first base. Tommy Paladino, behind the dish, and C.J. Mancini, right center. C.J. and Jake, we only have eight, so that means two outfielders. Lots of ground to cover out there."

Jake shot the boy a leery glance, not sure what to expect from the wiry newcomer.

"Don't worry, Jake," said Mac. "C.J. has been Coach Mac tested. You two will be fine out there. Just make sure you communicate and help each other out."

The boy knew he was batting last and playing right center field because he was the new guy, and not because he was a liability. He also knew the other guys on the team had every right to have a "wait and see" attitude about him. They were down a man, and he was a question mark. He would have felt the same way if he would have been back home at the Plaza and some new kid showed up halfway through the season. The one thing he had going for him was that he was not taking a position away from some other kid. In fact, he was saving the team from a loss just by showing up.

Lincoln and Rudy made their way out along the left field to warm up and the rest of the boys hit the field for pregame infield and outfield practice. As they trotted to the outfield, Jake saddled up next to the boy.

"Hey new guy, where'd you come from?"

"Pittsburgh," he said.

"Oh yeah, what part?"

"Oakland. It's where Forbes Field is, and Pitt."

"I know where it is. My brother goes to school there at Carnegie Tech. And we go to a Bucco game a couple times a year," said Jake.

The boy nodded and for a fleeting moment missed the old neighborhood.

"So, listen C.J., you ever play a night game before?"

In his excitement at the opportunity to play on the amazing field, the thought had never crossed his mind.

"Uh, no. I've never even seen another little league field with lights."

"Thought so. I've played here my whole life. It ain't much different but on high fly balls, you have to make sure you don't look right into the lights. Block them with your glove or hand or whatever you need to do. You have to track the ball right off the bat, too. If you do that, you'll be fine. Oh, and if one goes really high and it goes above the lights, it will disappear for a couple of seconds. Don't panic. Hold your ground and wait. But if you lose track of it, just wave your arms like a nut and I'll come over. And you help me out, too. Got it?"

"Yeah man. Thanks," C.J. said.

They split into their positions and for the first time in a while, the boy felt like everything was okay. The smell of freshly cut grass. The feel of soft leather on the palm of his hand. The crack of the ball against Coach Mac's fungo bat. He didn't have a word for it, but he knew it felt good.

As the infielders took grounders and threw the ball around the horn, the boy assessed the talent and figured the team to be as good as the ones back in Oakland, even better than some. After he and Jake both caught a couple of fly balls and threw to second and then third base, he knew that between the two of them, they could cover the outfield.

The Cardinals warmed up and after what seemed like two hours, the game finally got underway. After an uneventful first inning for both teams in the field and at the plate, the boy was hoping to get some swings in the bottom of the second inning. Rudy Meyers started the inning with a single into left field, but Bobby Rich flew out to center field for the first out. Covetti's first pitch to Freddy McGee skipped past the Cardinal catcher, Zeke Timmons, and Rudy moved up to second base.

This brought some chatter from the Orioles bench and the boy could feel his blood bubbling as he waited for his turn to bat.

McGee laced a hard one-hopper right at the second baseman, who checked on Rudy at second, then easily threw to first for the second out of the inning.

As the boy approached the plate, Coach Mac took a few steps towards him from the third base coaching box and with a wink and a clap, said, "Nothing to wait for C.J., bring him in."

The O's bench was alive and eager to see what the new kid could do.

"Bring him in Ceej..."

"Come on now new guy, you got this. Piece of cake."

The boy stepped into the batter's box as the umpire bellowed, "PLAY BALL!"

The Cardinals were in full force chattering away as well.

"Hey, batter batter, hey batter batter…"

Covetti delivered a decent fastball about a foot outside. One ball. No strikes.

Timmons, who stood a good six inches taller than the boy and most of the kids on the field for that matter, smacked his catcher's mitt with a fist and said, "Come on, Tony, blow it by him. He's looking for a walk!"

Covetti's next pitch was a little bit outside, but the boy measured it, connected and hit a blistering shot into the gap between the center fielder and right fielder. The ball skipped to the fence on one bounce and as Rudy easily scored from second base, the umpire chuckled and said, "I guess he wasn't lookin' for a walk after all, Zeke."

The boy trotted into second base standing up, the Orioles bench alive with hoots and hollers. As he stood with his hands on hips, he knew at that moment, he was part of the team.

The game rolled along, and the Orioles added two more runs to their lead, although Zeke exacted a bit of revenge when he tagged a home run over the scoreboard and into the town square in the fourth inning, a routine occurrence according to Jake.

And Smitty was as good as advertised. In the fourth inning, The boy was able to beat out a grounder between short and third, but no other Oriole had been able to catch up to Smitty's heat.

Then, in the top of the sixth inning, the boy did something that no kid had done against Smitty the entire season. With one ball and no strikes, the boy dug in, anticipating straight up fast balls. There were no surprises. Smitty threw hard and was able to just blow it by nearly every kid in the league.

As the next pitch buzzed towards the inside corner of the strike zone, the boy uncoiled and connected, sending the ball like a rocket into the air. Everyone watched, stunned, as it sailed well over the right field fence, but curled just outside the foul pole.

Few had hit the ball out of the infield on Smitty, and the new kid hit a rocket out of the park.

From the Cardinals dugout, Coach Kowalski shot a look of amazement at Coach Mac down the third base line and said, "shake it off Smitty. Just a long strike."

He then turned to assistant coach Bernie Smith, Smitty's dad and proprietor of Smitty's Bakery, and added,

"Longest damn foul ball I've seen a kid hit, let alone against your boy."

Bernie chuckled and said, "I should give that kid the baker's dozen just for that shot. Holy smokes!"

The boy knew he had poked the bear, so he resolved to let the next pitch go, no matter what, and it blew by him right down the middle of the plate. On the next pitch, the boy managed to lace a single into right field.

The Orioles went on to win by one run and the boy was three for three on the day at the plate, with two of his hits and an earth shattering foul ball coming against the almost unhittable Bernard "Smitty" Smith, Jr.

The new kid had indeed arrived in the Laurel Point Little League.

After the teams exchanged post-game handshakes, Smitty and Zeke stopped the boy at home plate.

"Hey man, nice stick. Good thing that blast went foul. I thought Smitty here was gonna cry," Zeke said.

"Shut up, Zeke!"

Smitty shook his head and asked, "Where'd you learn to hit like that?"

"I don't know, my old league was pretty good. Lots of good players. My coach knew a lot about hitting I guess."

Smitty said, "Man, we sure could use you against Davisburg on the Fourth for sure."

"When'd you move here?" Zeke asked.

The boy said, "A few days ago. Up near the drive-in, off the Bypass."

"Oh yeah? I live out that way on Warner Road," Zeke said.

Coach Mac waved, whistled, and called out from the third base dugout.

"Orioles, bring it in, bring it in."

The boy turned to the bench and nodded over his shoulder at Zeke and Smitty, "See you guys later."

The team sat on the bench facing Mac in nearly the same order as they had before the game.

"O's, a couple of things. First of all, big win! Proud of you all. C.J. way to make a first impression! Big team effort out there playing shorthanded."

Mac tamped down the boys hooting and hollering with a wave of the hand.

"As you know, the second all-star game of the year against Davisburg is right here on the Fourth of July, well on the third this year. You guys voted for Jake, Rudy and Bobby as our representatives before the game on Memorial Day. But here's the thing, Bobby has to go out of town. His great grandmother died, and he has to go to Harrisburg for the funeral."

Before anyone could react, Bobby said, "She was literally like a hundred years old. Like ninety nine. So, it's sad, but kind of not really sad, you know."

"Well," Coach continued, "we're all sorry for your loss all the same, Bob."

Jake asked, "So now what, Coach Mac? Do we still get a third player?"

"Well, yeah. We still get three because we were in the championship last season. So, just like the first time, I'm gonna leave that up to you guys. We're gonna vote."

Freddy McGee, who usually followed the don't speak unless spoken to rule, spoke.

"Coach Mac, before we vote, I'd like to say we haven't won a game against Davisburg in like twenty years, right? And, I mean, it's all those kids talk about."

"That's true, Freddy. It's been a long time," said Mac.

In fact, Laurel Point had zero wins and thirty seven losses against Davisburg over the past twenty seasons, with two games mercifully canceled due to rain.

The games in recent years had been closer and if not for a bad hop here and there and an inch or two difference along the foul line, Laurel Point would have won the last two.

Mac asked, "So Freddy, what are you trying to say?"

"I'm saying we're sick of losing and hearing about it at the pool and at church and everywhere else. I know C.J. is brand new. We don't stand a chance without Bobby, unless we pick C.J."

The thing about Freddy's "Don't speak unless spoken to" credo is when he did speak, the other kids listened. They knew if he was piping up, he had something good to say. Adults, too. He just had a contemplative way about him, and nearly everyone sensed it. He was one of the smartest kids in the class, never got in any scraps, and he played first base and hit the ball well enough that he was definitely next in line to go to make the All-Star team.

But the losing streak against Davisburg hung over Laurel Point like a black cloud. And it wasn't just around Memorial Day and every Fourth of July, although that is when it was strongest. It was year-round.

As sad as it sounds, it wasn't just the kids. The Davisburg adults had an arrogant air about them too. At the Rotary Club meetings, at the new strip mall on the highway between the towns, and even down at the American Legion. The folks from Davisburg took a patronizing tone when talking about the poor ball players from Laurel Point.

Coach Mac removed his cap and swatted it in Freddy's general direction. He gestured towards Coach Will, who was already ripping a page out of the back of the scorebook.

"Thanks for your input, Freddy. So, we put it to a vote. Secret ballot, names on a piece of paper, fold it up and hand it to Coach Will."

Coach Will distributed the paper and a fat number two pencil (compliments of Kwik-Towne Supermarket), passed from one boy to another until all eight had voted and handed the torn and folded pieces back to him.

Less than a minute later, pencil back behind his ear, Will announced the results.

"Seven votes for C.J. Mancini. One for Freddy McGee."

The boys, including Freddy, cheered, surrounded the boy as if he was Roberto Clemente himself, as he smiled from ear to ear.

Coach Mac smiled on the inside and remained stoic on the outside.

"Alright then, men. Jake, Rudy, and C.J., back here on Saturday at noon ready to play. Remember, the game is on July third because Independence Day falls on a Sunday this year. The rest of you guys, come down and support the team. It is time to break the streak!"

After another couple of minutes, the crowd dispersed and the players went their separate ways, the boy quietly left the dugout and headed back out the Bypass road blissfully and purposely undetected.

As Coach Mac moved through the exiting crowd, he stopped Rudy Meyers and asked, "Rudy, have you seen C.J.?"

"No Coach. Linc, did you see C.J.?"

Lincoln turned and said, "Yeah, he said he was going home with one of the guys on the Cards who lives out his way."

Coach Mac shook his head and said, "Okay. Thanks, fellas. Good game."

***

On Saturday, as the sun rose on Laurel Point, Smitty's dad shook him from a solid sleep and the two descended the back stairs of their second floor apartment to the bakery.

Smitty did this every weekend, usually assisting in icing cupcakes or filling lady locks. On this day, Bernie the Baker would be finishing up dozens upon dozens of his red, white, and blue sprinkled sugar cookies in preparation for the weekend's celebration. And even though he usually put his son to work, he knew they were both too preoccupied with the upcoming game, so he told Smithy to take a powder.

"Go enjoy the morning air, kid. Otherwise, we'll just be in here yacking about the game and getting nothing done."

He handed Smitty a waxy white paper bag and said, "Here's a couple of bear claws for George. He ought to be rolling up soon."

Smitty did not have to be told twice. Bag in hand, he went out front and took a seat on the park bench passing the minutes, which felt like hours. He admired the morning sky, thanking the heavens for a clear, perfect day for baseball.

As the sun rose on Main Street, Smitty watched as the Pittsburgh Post-Gazette truck rambled up the block towards Martin's Five and Dime next door to the bakery. The driver, a burly man of about fifty years old wearing a sleeveless t-shirt, navy blue work pants, and army boots eased the truck into the wide open spot in front of the store and hopped out onto the sidewalk.

He waved a hello to Smitty as he moved quickly to the back of the truck, opened the liftgate and dropped a bundle of twenty five morning papers near the front door of Martin's.

With the task at hand behind him, he asked, "How's it going, young Mr. Smith?"

"So far, so good, George. How are you?"

"Eh, just trying to get through the run and back home for the holiday weekend. Big cookout tomorrow. Got sixteen people coming over."

"Sounds like fun."

"Mostly. But I do all the grillin' and everybody has an opinion. Other than that, it is a great day. Weather is supposed to be good, too. Big game today, huh?"

"Yeah. Hopin' to break the streak."

"Well, between you, me, and the telly pole, I sure as hell hope you do it, kid. I've been hearing about it for years over there."

Smitty laughed and said, "Thanks, George. Oh, yeah, almost forgot. Here's a couple of bear claws for you. Happy Fourth."

"Ah, thanks Smitty. Best dang pastry from here to Pittsburgh, and believe me, I've sampled 'em all!"

George climbed back in the driver's seat, saluted Smitty and said, "Go get 'em today, kid. I got a good feelin'."

Smitty laughed and nodded as George started up the truck and took off down Main towards the Bypass road.

As was his Saturday custom, Smitty wiggled a newspaper free from the middle of the wire bound bundle and eased himself back onto the park bench to have a look at the previous day's box scores.

He unfolded the paper and shot back up from the bench as he saw it at the bottom of page one, in the bottom right corner below *LBJ Announces Plans for Teachers' Corps* and *Pittsburghers Warned Of Holiday Dangers*. A two paragraph article complete with a photograph. He read through it once, studied the photo, and muttered something that would cost him at least a two dollar donation to his mother's swear jar upstairs.

Without so much as a second thought, Smitty tore off the corner of the page, stuffed it into his pocket, grabbed the bundle of newspapers by the wire, wedged the loose paper back into the bunch, and hustled through the walkway between the bakery and Martin's to the back alley.

He jumped on his bike and guided himself down the alley gaining enough speed to hold the handlebars with his right hand and the bundle of newspapers in his left, at his side.

Smitty pedaled furiously, stopping only once, to toss the bundle into the big dumpster behind Wesley's Auto Parts just before the turn-off to the Bypass.

When he arrived at the Kwik-Towne Supermarket, Smitty was relieved to see the two bundles of Post-Gazette newspapers sitting against a fleet of shopping carts near the door. And not a person in sight inside the store, or in the lot. Being a third generation early-riser could be a pain, but it also had its benefits.

He somehow managed to once again carry a bundle in his left hand, but also added another bundle to his lap as he pedaled away from the strip mall parking lot and around back as far from the Kwik-Towne as possible without leaving the mall.

Sweat forming on his brow as he covered the bundles with rug scraps, two by fours and carpet padding in the dumpster behind Lyle's Carpet and Flooring, Smitty was glad only two places in Laurel Point sold the Pittsburgh Post-Gazette. He knew this from his many Saturday morning conversations with George, who freely admitted that he had bid on the longer, but less strenuous route "out to the country" to take it easy on his shoulders and back.

George, about every other week, would say, "Less stops means less tossin' the bundles, less wear and tear on the bad shoulder. Plus, the scenery is nice, and the pastries are second to none!"

Once back at the bakery, Smitty wanted to go nowhere near the front of the store for fear of questions from Mr. Martin, so he quietly made his way to the back room, donned a white apron, and began sweeping the floors in silence.

***

The town square bustled with folks excited for the weekend's festivities. Aside from the game, there would be fireworks on the third AND Fourth, free dogs and burgers (compliments of Levinson Meats and the Kwik-Towne Supermarket!) all weekend at the ball field AND in the square, clowns, bands, one-act plays depicting our nation's history on the main stage presented by the Green Barn Community Players, and so much more. Losing streak aside, the fine people of Laurel Point loved a good celebration. Davisburg may have won a lot of ball games, but when it came to putting on a festival, nobody beat Laurel Point.

A carnival atmosphere swallowed up the town as the teams warmed up on the immaculate field just a block away and there was a little extra anticipation in the air. The boys had been getting oh so close. On the doorstep of victory in the last couple of meetings. The townsfolk knew it. They felt it. And they had all heard about this new boy who might just be able to nudge them past Davisburg. This phenom.

At the field, the teams assembled on their respective benches and Coach Mac, as he had done a little less than two days earlier, introduced the new boy to the team. But this time, every kid on that bench had heard of C.J. from the Orioles.

Billy Roma, the Yankees' representative, got the razzing started.

"Hey Smitty, did you need a neck brace from strainin' your neck watchin' that ball get over the fence so fast?"

Not to be outdone, Lance Archer from the Phillies added, "Yeah man, I heard that ball landed two zip codes over."

Smitty knew it was coming and to be fair, had no problem with it. But he did feel the need to defend his honor.

"Arch, you ain't had a hit off me since we were eight years old, so..."

"Okay guys," said Coach Kowalski, "let's get down to business. Coach Mac, line-up. Please."

Mac stepped up and read off the starting nine and their positions. This time, among the best players in the league, the boy was slotted sixth in the order. They knew he should be batting lead-off or second but had made a concession to the fact that he had only played one game in the league. He was also penciled in as the right fielder. This at first glance seemed to be because he was a new player, and it would certainly look that way to the uninitiated. But the coaches knew that two of Davisburg's biggest hitters were lefties and most of their right handed hitters would have trouble getting around on Pat McTighe's fastball and especially Smitty's heat. What could be a lonely position was sure to get lots of action today.

The game proved to be an exciting back and forth affair just as the last couple of meetings had been. The boy patrolled right field like his idol and what he didn't track down, Jake in center field had covered. Smitty had tossed three innings, giving up only two hits. It looked to the boy like Smitty had been throwing even harder than the previous game. The boy tallied a single, a double, two stolen bases and had scored one of Laurel Point's two runs.

Davisburg, as usual, was a machine. Garnering three runs over five innings, scoring one in the fourth off of Sam Tellerman from the A's and two in the fifth off of McTighe to take the lead going into the sixth.

At the end of the fifth inning, Coach Kingman, after some persuading from Coach Mac, approached the boy in the dugout.

"C.J., how's your arm feel?"

"Um, great Coach."

"I'm out of fresh arms. Well, real good ones, anyway. Smitty, Sammy, and Pat held them down pretty good. You think you can do the same?"

The boy looked the coach in the eye and said, "Absolutely."

The boy trotted out to the mound, knowing he would be facing the top of the Davisburg batting order. It was as if he had lived for this moment his entire life. No butterflies in his belly. No apprehension.

After the boy threw his warm-up pitches, Rudy over at shortstop took a few steps towards him and said, "You got this, C.J., Just like the other night."

The boy removed his cap and wiped the sweat from his brow as the umpire tossed him a brand new ball for the sixth and final inning.

Smitty approached from first base and said, "Hey man. We got your back. Every one of us out here. We got your back."

The boy felt the gravity of Smitty's words, as if he was talking about more than just a baseball game on a sunny summer day.

Twelve pitches later, the boy had mowed down the first two Davisburg hitters like they were tee-ballers and had overwhelmed the number three man in their order with an inside fastball that he was able to fight off just enough to hit a lazy ground ball to first that Smitty fielded easily for the third out.

Laurel Point had one last chance to score a run to force extra innings or score two to win, with the meat of their order coming to the plate. Tommy Dwyer from the Red Sox got things moving with a single to left field. Chip Nevers from the Pirates grounded to short, forcing Tommy out at second. Chip, who was running faster than he had ever done in his life, was determined not to let Davisburg get the double play, beating the throw from second by two steps. One down, one on.

Smitty, feeling the adrenaline pumping through his body, blasted a foul ball line drive almost as far as the boy's had gone a couple of days earlier, then laced the next pitch into right center for a double. Second and third one out.

Could this be the hit that breaks the streak? Billy Roma, filled with maybe more adrenaline than Smitty and not one to let a good pitch go by, smashed the first offering on a line, but directly at the short stop. Out number two.

Laurel Point was down to their final chance. Two men in scoring position.

The boy approached the plate in a scene that looked like it had been written for a Hollywood movie. Nearly the whole town was at the game, and the folks who had been in the town square were now lined up two or three deep along the outfield fence. All of this for a game played by eleven and twelve year old boys.

The Laurel Point bench chattered. The Davisburg bench chattered. The boy choked up slightly on the bat and stepped into the batter's box. No nerves. No anxiety. Just resolve.

The first pitch looked to the boy to be a few inches outside, but the umpire, who had a tight strike zone the entire game, called it a strike. Nothing to wait for now, the boy thought.

From second base, Smitty cupped his hands and yelled, "Come on, kid. One good rip. We got your back."

The next pitch, just as the boy had hoped, was also a bit outside, but instead of risking going in the hole, he swung and laced a line drive to the left center field fence, easily scoring Chip from third and Smitty from second. The boy trotted into second base standing up and just like that, the streak was over. Laurel Point defeated Davisburg four to three, ending twenty years of futility.

The Laurel Point team mobbed the boy at second base as the crowd went wild.

Davisburg, to their credit, took the loss with their heads held high. After all, they have thirty seven wins and one loss in the last thirty eight games. And as their coach told both teams after the game, "It was an honor to be part of such a great baseball game. Now where are those hot dogs and sugar cookies?"

Coach Kingman, who had coached through most of the streak, was unable to speak after the game. So, Mike Tellerman, coach of the A's and vice-president of the Kiwanis Club did the honors.

"Boys, I'll be brief, which if you know me, that is hard to believe. But you should be proud of yourselves and proud of your town. We are proud of every last one of you! Now go enjoy the holiday weekend!"

Coach Mac looked at the boys and said, "I have nothing to add. Team effort. Great win. Go have fun."

As the field emptied and most folks made their way to the town square, Smitty, Jake, Rudy, and Zeke Timmons approached the boy.

"Hey man," Smitty said, "remember when I said we got your back?"

The boy looked at Smitty, happy, but puzzled.

"Yeah?"

He pulled the newspaper article from the back pocket of his uniform pants and showed it to the boy.

"You're front page news, kid," said Smitty.

Jake put his hand on the boy's shoulder and said, "Look man, whatever you need, like Smitty said, we got your back."

***

Early the next morning, as the sun rose over a jubilant Laurel Point, James Whaley, fourth generation funeral director at Johnson-Whaley Funeral Home, appeared on Mac's front porch and knocked at the wooden screen door. Mac's wife, Kate, answered the door with a twin toddler clinging to each leg.

"Morning, Kate. Is Mac home?"

Her startled look said all he needed to know.

"Oh, listen, Katie! It isn't anything bad! Nobody died! Happy Fourth of July by the way."

The young Mr. Whaley was still getting the hang of prefacing any visit that was not directly related to his family business with that caveat. Otherwise, people just looked at him as if he was a baby-faced grim reaper.

Katie's relief was palpable.

Mac walked across the living room and joined Katie at the door. As she turned back into the house, she said, "For the love of God, Jimmy. My heart was racing!"

"Hey, Jimmy, what's up? Great game yesterday, huh?"

"Tremendous, Mac. Proud of those boys. That's what I need to talk to you about."

"What do you mean, Jim?"

The coach ushered Jim towards the padded wicker chair and Mac took a seat on the porch swing.

"Your new kid, Did I hear them say his name is C.J. Mancini? And he's from Oakland down in Pittsburgh?"

"Yeah, why?"

"Well see, last year when I was finishing up mortuary school in Pittsburgh, Oakland as a matter of fact, I had a job at a place down there, Dawson Brothers Funeral Home."

Perplexed, Mac looked at Jimmy and said, "Okay, go on."

"Well, we had a kid by that same name, Carl Joseph Mancini, that we buried. They called him C.J. It was the saddest dang thing I ever went through. Poor kid had cancer. It almost made me go back to school for accounting or some dang thing."

Mac was stunned but he did not speak.

"The other thing is," Jimmy continued, "I'm pretty sure your new kid was one of his best friends."

Mac, still stunned, felt a lump of guilt in his chest.

"But he had a valid birth certificate. A real one."

"Born on New Year's Day?"

"YES! How do you know that?"

Jimmy shook his head and said, "I took care of having the prayer cards printed. Born on New Year's Day. Died on Halloween. You don't forget those dates."

"I should have checked up on him a little more. Done more due diligence. But... well then who is this kid?"

"I don't remember his name. I can give Paul Dawson a call later today to see if he can shed some light."

"Well, C.J., or whoever he really is, said he's staying out by the Bypass with his grandparents."

Jimmy cocked his head and asked the obvious question.

"But if he moved in with his grandparents, why use a fake name? And how did he get C.J.'s birth certificate?"

"Good question. Maybe he is too old for our league? Maybe he doesn't have one of his own? Jeez. I'm grasping at straws here."

As if out of thin air, Bernie the Baker and Smitty appeared on the front steps. As usual, Bernie held in his hand a white paper bag.

Bernie had learned never to show up unannounced at someone's home, or anywhere for that matter, without something from the bakery. A loaf of bread. A bar cake. Maybe a coffee cake. And in this case, a half dozen of those very same bear claws that George the Post-Gazette driver raves about from Laurel Point to Pittsburgh.

"Morning gents. Up early on this fine day, I see," Bernie said.

Mac stood and waved the two onto the porch and said, "Hello Bernie. Smitty. Come on up and have a seat."

As Smitty joined Coach Mac on the porch swing, Katie emerged from the house.

"Hello Bernie. Hello Smitty. Seems the MacNeil house is the most popular place in town this morning."

Bernie handed the bag to Katie and said, "Good morning, Kate. Brought you some bear claws, and a couple of thumb prints for the little ones."

"Well, thank you so much Bernie!"

Kate retreated into the house as Bernie took a seat opposite Jimmy. He waved towards Smitty and said, "Son, go ahead and show Coach Mac what you got there."

Smitty slid the torn article from his pocket, unfolded it, and handed it to Mac.

As Mac accepted it by the tattered edge, he said. "I knew this visit wasn't just about those bear claws."

There in black and white, between *Crafton Girl Becomes Nun* and *Montefiore Gives Dr. Segel A Post* was a headline that jumped off the page and formed a lump in Mac's throat.

Oakland Boy Missing from Edgewood Orphanage.

"Holy shi...DANG!"

He read the short article aloud.

"Eleven year old Joseph Cronin from the Oakland neighborhood disappeared from the Holy Spirit Orphanage in Edgewood last Friday. The boy had last been seen within the walls of the facility around the dinner hour. At dusk, Lois Kratz, of Swissvale, who was walking her dog near her home on Roslyn Street at Waverly Street, saw a boy carrying a duffle bag fitting Cronin's description heading east along the

railroad tracks. Anyone with information is directed to call the Edgewood Borough Police Department..."

The school photo of the boy left no doubt.

Stunned, Mac looked up from the article, tears welling in his eyes.

Bernie nodded towards his son.

"Go on, Bernard, tell him the rest."

Jimmy shot up.

"That's it! Cronin. Joe Cronin. He was C.J.'s best buddy. Took his death real hard, too. Like I said, Mac, it almost made me quit the business, it was so sad."

Smitty glanced at Jimmy, wondering how he knew about the real C.J.

"He was staying in the Buford's old house off the Bypass. It's empty since Mrs. Buford moved out, but it has running water and electricity and all. He came upon it after he jumped off the train and figured he could stay there, at least for a little bit."

Mac and Jimmy were speechless and astonished that a kid could pull off such a thing.

Bernie said, "Think about it, fellas. There isn't another house within a quarter mile, so it was easy to sneak in and out, under the radar."

Smitty continued, "But Coach Mac, you don't need to worry about him. He went back. He asked me to give this to you. I think it explains things pretty good."

Smitty handed Mac a number ten envelope with a crooked Smitty's Bakery rubber stamp in the top left corner. The coach pulled a single piece of loose leaf paper from the envelope and read silently.

After about thirty seconds, which felt more like an hour to everyone besides Mac, Jimmy said, "What's it say, Mac? I mean if you want to tell us, that is."

Mac cleared his throat, nodded, and wiped his cheek.

"Dear Coach, I'm sorry I wasn't honest with you but all I wanted to do was play ball. C.J. was a real person, though. He was my best friend. He died. His mom gave me a shoe box with some of his things in it like baseball cards and an article about Maz. That's how I got his birth record. I don't think that was supposed to be in the box. Anyway, some of what I told you is true. My father died and my mother had to go to a mental hospital. So, then I had to go to a home for boys. I don't have grandparents or any other family as far as I know. Sorry I was not honest about that. The truth is, I walked out of the orphan home and jumped a train. Don't worry. I am going to jump

the train and go back. I feel bad because Sister Mary Benedict is a nice lady, and I don't want her to worry or feel bad because I ran away. I knew it couldn't last, even though I wanted it to.

Thank you for letting me feel like I am part of a team. I kept the uniform. I hope that is ok. Sincerely, Joe Cronin."

As Kate set a tray of bear claws and a pot of coffee on the table, she said, "Goodness, we have to call that orphanage to see if he made it."

"No need Katie," said Bernie.

Smitty said, "Yeah, Joe called me this morning from the orphanage. I gave him our phone number before he jumped the train. That nun got on the phone too, so we know he was back. I think she wanted to be mad at him, but she just really seemed to be relieved he was safe and back there."

Bernie shook his head.

"Well, Bernard, Jake, Rudy, and Zeke made sure he got on the train back towards Pittsburgh. Obviously, they should have told some grownups, and one of us could have given him a proper ride back, but..."

Smitty interrupted his dad.

"We just didn't want him to get in trouble, like maybe get thrown in juvie with a bunch of delinquents, is all. He said the place wasn't so bad, and he is back there now, so that's what matters to us. None of us ever met a kid like that before. Like, not just about baseball, either. We could never even imagine going through what he's been through, so we had his back."

Coach Mac said, "Well, in the end, you boys did right by him, Smitty. We all just hope he's okay."

Smitty lifted a bear claw off the plate, shook his head, smiled and said, "He'll be okay, Coach. Better than okay, even. He's a phenom."

The Gate

Patrick Mannion walked the long wooden city steps that connected Bates Street with Frazier Street, among the steady line of weary laborers making their way back up the hill. The more hours in the mill, the more steps there seemed to be.

As he made his way along one of the endless landings between flights, the pitter-pattering of the soft rain against the leaves and mud along the hillside reminded him of home. He closed his eyes and wished himself back, at least for the moment, to the hills of Connemara, walking on the road to Tourmakeady in the misty drizzle.

On those rainy days, he'd hurry along, knowing she would not be there. On sunny days he would walk slowly and deliberately, hoping to see Sarah Ronan at the gate of the whitewashed thatched cottage overlooking the lake.

Each day along the way, he would plan his greeting in anticipation. Some days he would nod and say, "Good day, Sarah." Sometimes he would wave and say, "How are ye keepin' Miss Ronan?" Once in a while, he would tip his cap but say nothing. A trick he had learned from his grandfather. He figured the old man had outlived three wives, so he must have known something about the affairs of the heart. But every day he would smile. There was no need to plan that part. The mere sight of her brought a smile.

On days when she was alone, he could be sure of a return greeting. She might say, "Well hello, Mr. Mannion." Or "I'm well, Patrick. Thank you." On days when her father was in the doorway or within earshot, Patrick could count on a smile, but no words. And that was just fine with him.

The mill over the hill belched a flame high into the gray sky and the smell of sulfur jolted him back to the reality that he was far from the west of Ireland. Far from the road to Tourmakeady. And far from Sarah Ronan waiting at the gate.

The Irish Sports Page

"Brother Jerome will see you now, Regis."

"Thank you, Mrs. Davis."

He placed the newspaper back on the end table, stood up, walked by the reception counter, nodded at a smiling Mrs. Davis, and tapped on the varnished door jam.

"Come in, Mr. Ahearn," directed a calming but authoritative voice.

"Thank you, Brother," he said as he approached the small wooden desk.

Two leather chairs that had seen better days sat opposite the desk, which was one step up from a regular old classroom teacher's desk. This surprised Regis.

"Have a seat."

Brother Jerome gestured from behind the desk towards the worn leather chairs and Regis dutifully sat down, facing the Vice Principal for Academic Affairs for the first time in his short Central Catholic High School career.

Gold wire rimmed glasses framed Brother Jerome's thin face. He was balding and had recently given in and had his graying hair cut close to his smooth scalp.

On the desk was a rickety lamp, an immaculate "At a Glance" blotter calendar - compliments of Parkvale Savings Bank, a cup holding three pencils and two ball point pens, a nameplate with *Bro. Jerome Cyrankiewicz, F.S.C.* etched on it, a black touch tone phone, and a brand new manilla folder, with "Ahearn, Regis – 1F 411" typed on the tab. No chachkies or knick knacks, not even a small religious statue.

The walls of the office were adorned with dull, framed prints of Renaissance and Impressionists paintings and the requisite portrait of St. John Baptist de La Salle, founder of the Christian Brothers. All hung no doubt decades earlier and moved once every five years or so to paint the walls. The only recent addition, hanging by a single nail, was a small Diocese of Pittsburgh calendar.

It was clear to Regis that Brother Jerome was not one for frills or adding a "personal touch" to his work environment. The only signs of Brother Jerome in the room was the actual Brother Jerome, and the nameplate sitting on his desk.

"So, Mr. Ahearn, you are Kevin's brother?"

"Yes."

"And Sean's as well?"

"Yes, Brother."

"And Hugh's?"

"Yes, and Tice, uh, short for Terrence, Thomas, Brian, Patrick, and Christos."

Brother Jerome smirked, nodded, and said, "Thank you."

"No problem. I figured I'd save you the time."

Regis felt a little more at ease after the requisite roll call of the nine Ahearn boys.

"You forgot Mary Ellen and Colleen."

"Oh, I thought we were just naming my brothers since, you know, the girls didn't go here," Regis said.

Brother Jerome chuckled again and said, "Fair enough, Mr. Ahearn. But they both did the spring musicals, so that counts right? I am curious, where did the name Christos come from?"

"It's Greek," said Regis.

Brother Jerome cocked his head and said, "I know it's Greek, son. That's why I am asking."

"Oh yeah, right. Well, my dad was overseas with a guy from Chicago by the name of Christos Papademos. They promised each other when they got home and went their separate ways and got married, if they ever had kids, my dad would name a boy after Christos and he would name a boy after my dad, Patrick. Except my dad's given name is Padraig, which is real Irish. But he told Christos he would settle for Patrick. So that's why I have a brother with a Greek first name."

"I see. So is there..."

"Yes. Christos held up his end of the bargain. There is a guy out in Chicago by the name of Patrick Nicholas Papademos. Pat Papademos."

Brother Jerome laughed out loud, shook his head and said, "Fair enough. Your brother Christos graduated before I came back to Central, so I never knew that. Makes perfect sense."

Regis waited, not knowing whether they were finished with the introductory sibling talk.

"So, Regis. What can I do for you?"

"Um, well Brother, my grandmother died."

"I see. I'm very sorry for your loss."

"Thank you. And like, it's finals week and she's being laid out, um, today and tomorrow and, um, the funeral is Friday morning, so, uh…"

Brother Jerome studied Regis, and the young man figured the Vice Principal was looking for a crack or a tell.

"Mr. Ahearn, how many grandmothers do you have?"

Regis, puzzled by the question, said, "Um, two, Brother. Well, none now. I had two to start with. My dad's mother died a long time ago, when I was three. And, well, this one, she died on Monday."

"So, no step-grandmothers?"

He asked the question, fully knowing the answer.

"No, Brother."

"No close family friends that you consider to be a grandmother?"

"Uh, no sir. Why do you ask?"

"Because by my recollection, this is your fourth grandmother to pass away."

Regis was blindsided.

"Maybe you have us mixed up with the Saint James Ahearns from Wilkinsburg, Brother. We're cousins. So, they have two and we have two, which equals four. Grandmothers, that is."

Brother Jerome again cocked his head and asked, "But if you're cousins, wouldn't you share a grandmother? Making it a total of three?"

"No. Second cousins, so different grandmothers."

"I see. Point taken, But rest assured, Mr. Ahearn, this is the fourth report of a dead grandmother in the Saint Agnes, Buffalo Street Ahearn family in my recollection."

Regis began to connect some dots. As the youngest of the eleven Ahearn children, it had been necessary for him to live down the less than savory behavior of a couple of his brothers on a few occasions. He, in a matter of seconds, even had some suspects in mind.

"Brother, I can, um, assure you, my grandmother is dead, currently. And I can also assure you she is only my second grandmother to die. Like I said, my other one died when I was three, so twelve years ago."

Brother Jerome was in no hurry to interject, so Regis continued.

"So, probably Tommy and Brian were here, then. Maybe Tice. That was my dad's mother that died, like I said."

Brother nodded and sat, elbows on the desk, hands clasped, but said nothing, presumably allowing Regis to sink or swim.

"So, that's all the grandmothers, Brother."

Regis had already eliminated Christos, Tommy, Brian, and Sean from his list of perpetrators. They were by no means angels, but Christos was all business, Tommy and Brian would have been too afraid to lie about something so close to home, and if Sean wanted to get out of school, he would just cut. No note, no plan. Which is the main reason Mrs. Ahearn had to practically beg Brother Boniface, when he had called with the news that Brian would not be invited back for his senior year, to give Sean one more chance. Sean, to his credit, ended up making it through by the skin of his teeth.

Regis could see Tice and Kevin making up a dead grandmother story. Definitely. Maybe Patrick, but probably not. He had been good at leaving all his shenanigans, and there had been plenty, for outside the walls of Central Catholic. But Hughie wouldn't just make up a story, he'd add details, possibly sad, possibly gory.

After spending a few seconds internally running down his suspect pool, Regis had a thought.

"Hold on Brother. I'll be right back."

He rose and went back to the outer office and grabbed the Pittsburgh Post-Gazette from the end table.

He returned to the office and placed the paper on the desk in front of Brother Jerome.

"It will be in there. Right in the Irish Sports Page."

Brother Jerome looked at Regis with a bewildered grin and asked, "The Irish Sports Page?"

"Yeah, you know, the death notices. That's what my dad calls it, because every Irish person around goes straight to the death notices, like other people go straight to the sports page."

Brother laughed and shook his head as he flipped through to the classifieds and finally the death notices.

"What's the name, Regis?"

"Oh, yeah. Right. Dornan. Mary Bridget Dornan."

There, in black and white, was the death notice of Mary Bridget Dornan (nee Coyne), age 92, of Oakland, originally of Westport, County Mayo Ireland. Listed among her rather large family were all twenty seven grandchildren by name. Regis was twenty-seventh.

"Well then, Mr. Ahearn, they saved the best for last. Thank you for clearing that up for me. The Brothers will offer up their evening prayers for your family. She leaves quite a legacy. You will be excused from the tests and will have the opportunity to make them up next week upon your return to school."

"You're welcome, Brother. And thank you."

Brother Jerome rose as Regis did the same.

"Mr. Ahearn, offer my condolences to your family."

With a wink, he continued, "Especially Kevin and Hugh."

The Reward

She slid the plate across the Formica countertop towards the unassuming man in the rumpled tweed jacket.

"Here ya go Feeney. The usual."

He nodded and thanked her, in a voice barely above a whisper.

'The usual' consisted of two eggs, over medium, two slices of rye toast, and a side of fried potatoes. Unless it was Friday. Then it was French toast with a side of bacon. Always a cup of coffee. No need to top it off more than once. Black.

He visited the diner every weekday except Thursday. As far as she knew, he had never been in on a Saturday, but it was her day off, so she couldn't say for sure.

Carol Dolmak had been working the counter at The Craig Diner for twenty-four years and Feeney had been eating breakfast there for the past seventeen. She knew this because her Raymond had turned two years old the same day Feeney had taken a seat at the end of the counter for the first time. She had no idea why she put the two things together.

Feeney was usually not much for conversation and Carol was fine with that. The counter crowd made enough jibber jabber, and he was respectful, polite, and left an eighteen percent tip after every visit. This is not to say he was awkward or aloof. On the contrary. He was, by his own admission, more of an observer than a contributor. But when he did make conversation with the other counter regulars or interlopers, he was interesting, obviously intelligent, and warm. In that way, Carol found him to be an enigma.

She had often wished he would add more to the usual hum drum conversation of the breakfast crowd. But she also had a fierce code of respect for any visitor to her counter. No nosey questions. If someone wanted to go on and on about their daughter's new boyfriend or their pain in the you-know-what boss, they would do it on their own terms. Not hers. After all, folks were mostly there to have a nice hot meal. Carol was not one for gossip. She liked it when people shared the happy things, and she was more than willing to reciprocate.

But if someone was having a bad day, or needed to get something off their chest, she was there to lend a sympathetic ear. She was not there to solve the world's problems, but over the years she had developed a sense for when to listen and when to chime in.

She and Feeney were alike in that way. But one thing was for sure, she knew not much more about the slight man in the tweed jacket than she had seventeen years ago. She did not know if Feeney was his first or last name. She figured him to be somewhere between sixty-five and eighty years old, and he seemingly hadn't aged a day in seventeen years. She knew he had never married, and he had never mentioned any extended family in more than just vague terms, and in the past tense. Carol had no idea where he lived. She knew from context clues that he was retired, but she had no idea what he had done for a living. She had never seen him outside the Craig Diner. She had never bumped into him on the street or in the Giant Eagle supermarket or at church with her family. He didn't look particularly well-off, but he didn't look destitute either. To Carol, he looked and acted like a regular, run of the mill type bachelor.

He had his quirks. His routines. His go-to expressions and silence fillers. All the regulars did. Although Feeney only used two on a regular basis.

When he walked in and took his seat at the counter, he would almost always say, "Hoo-boy. How about this weather?" He said it when it was raining. He said it when it was sunny and seventy-two degrees. He said it when it was twelve degrees and snowing.

Just about every day, after he had finished his breakfast, paid his bill and was readying himself for the aforementioned weather, he'd say to Carol, "Thank you dear. Someday you will be properly rewarded."

Those were his standards. During the in-between times when he sipped coffee and waited for his breakfast, he was usually just fine with silence, although once in a while when Carol would top him off, he'd throw in a "Not too busy today," or a "Lunch crowd seems to be coming in a little early."

He felt no need to fill the air with words about himself or his opinions on world affairs or the Steelers. He felt no need to ask personal questions of Carol or anyone else in the place. But it was clear to her that Feeney knew she had a husband and three children, two girls and a boy. She knew this because every year a couple of days before Christmas, he would add a crisp, new five dollar bill on top of his eighteen percent tip, and say, "You and Bill go buy something nice for the kids." With a wink, he'd add, "Provided they're on the good list."

On this Wednesday, Feeney ate in silence, as a couple of regulars at the other end of the counter yammered on and on about the Pirates prospects for the upcoming season. When he was done eating, he settled up and as he straightened his jacket and turned for the door, he waved to Carol as she placed a plate of French toast in front of a stranger at table three and said, "Ah, good choice, sir. Best French toast in all of Oakland. Pittsburgh, even. Thank you, Carol. Someday you will be properly rewarded."

And with that, Feeney left the Craig Diner, never to return.

Nearly two weeks later, Jimmy Bradley, who sat and read the Post-Gazette religiously at the opposite end of the counter from Feeney's perch, flicked the open paper with his middle finger and said, "I think we have our answer, right here, Hon."

Carol turned to Bradley as she waited for an order at the kitchen window and said, "Answer to what, Brad?"

"Where your man Feeney disappeared to."

Jimmy folded and flattened the paper and set it on the counter facing her. He pointed at the death notice and said, "Feeney. Suddenly on Thursday, April 16, Calvin A., of Oakland. That's probably him, right? Arrangements by H. Samson's, but no viewing or service. Interment at Allegheny Cemetery. Everything private. No family listed at all."

She ran her hand across the page and shook her head.

"Must be him. Sad, he had nobody. He never really mentioned anyone, but you never know if that's because a person has nobody, or just doesn't have anyone they really want to tell you about. Ya know what I mean?"

Bradley nodded.

"He kept to himself and all, but he seemed to be a decent man. Sorry about it all the same, Carol."

"Me too, Jimmy. Me too."

***

Two months had passed, and life had continued to roll on at the Craig Diner. But every time a stranger sat in Feeney's spot and ordered eggs over medium, she smiled at the thought of the gentleman in the rumpled tweed jacket.

On a lazy Friday morning, as the door opened and the bell clinked, Carol looked up from the register and said, "We don't open for five minutes, hon. You'll have to wait outside."

A tall, lean, man in a tailored charcoal suit held a business envelope and made his way directly to Feeney's stool and took a seat.

"I'm looking for a Mrs. George Dolmak. I apologize, Ma'am. This will only take a minute. Is Mrs. Dolmak here?"

Carol studied the stately stranger and spied her name and home address on the cream colored envelope.

"I'm Mrs. Dolmak. Carol Dolmak."

"It's a pleasure Mrs. Dolmak. I am Sanford Milligan, attorney for the Estate of Calvin A. Feeney. Did you know Mr. Feeney?"

"Well, he parked himself on that very seat four times a week for upwards of seventeen years, and I waited on him almost every one of those days, so I suppose I knew him well enough."

Milligan handed the envelope to Carol and said, "He wanted you to have this. He must have thought very highly of you."

Carol took the envelope and asked, "Me? What is it?"

"Well," said Mr. Milligan, "You'll just have to read the letter."

She said, "Feeney, he never really told me much of anything personal. He listened more than he talked, know what I mean?"

Milligan smiled like the cat that ate the canary.

"I do know what you mean. I do indeed. He had no living family. His parents were long gone. No siblings or other relatives. And he worked in the Fidelity Trust Building downtown for many years. Retired twenty years ago."

"So, he was a banker then?"

Milligan let out a knowing chuckle and said, "No, no. Not a banker. Never finished secondary school as a matter of fact. He was an elevator operator. He listened more than he talked in that elevator, too. For thirty-five years. He took it all in. Heard every word uttered by every banker and big shot in his elevator. And, well, let's just say it paid off for him."

Milligan stood and pointing at the envelope said, "I'll leave you to read that letter and the papers. My card is in there, too. Mr. Feeney allocated funds for my fees for any legal assistance you will need. And if I might be so forward, you are going to need an attorney. It is, well, it is, quite a bit, I'll just let you read the letter."

As the door clacked, the bell clanged, and Milligan disappeared onto the street. Carol tore open the envelope and read the letter *Re: Estate of Calvin A. Feeney*, on official Erikson, Milligan and Percival, P.C. letterhead. She fought through two paragraphs of legalese before uttering, "Jesus, Mary and Joseph! Oh, my word!"

She read it again. And again. And once again, to make sure her eyes were not playing tricks on her, adding zeros that weren't there. Her eyes were fine.

Nick, the morning manager, peered through the window between the counter and the kitchen and said, "Carol, you alright, hon? You look like you seen a ghost!"

As she headed for the door, she said, "Nicky, I'm not feeling so good. I, uh, I have to go home."

'Someday' had come. Carol had been properly rewarded.

Speak No Evil

As the cool late summer breeze pushes across the parking lot, a faraway wind chime and the smell of burgers on a charcoal grill take me back to bygone days. I walk up the concrete slope wondering how many times in my life I had gone through the ominous front door of this building. It is enough that I can mark the era by the color of the flapping awning hanging over the long porch. These days it is maroon with white trim. In my youth it was green. Bright green. When I was a younger man, it was black, eventually fading to gray. Really the only thing ominous about the door is the fact that it is the entrance to a funeral home. It is a beat up, plain white wooden door with a frosted window and a mail slot so low I am sure every letter carrier for the last six decades has complained about it. There is rarely anything good on the other side of the door. Grief, sadness, anger, tragedy, and maybe occasionally even relief.

I can tell the story now because Andrew "Hound" Bassett is on the other side of the door in a box, and I am the only one left. I suppose the real question is, do I want to tell the story.

A lot of people had theories about what had happened to Joseph Robert Bertram when he disappeared back in 1977. A lot of people had made plenty of claims about seeing him here or there, on the day he vanished and in the years that followed. A lot of people had plenty to say about his family. A lot of people had plenty to say about this neighbor, or that neighbor. A lot of people had phoned in so-called leads to the police station. All dead ends. All bullshit.

Forty-five years later, people are still trying to figure it out. The annual newspaper article on the anniversary of Joseph's disappearance rehashes the same thin set of well-worn facts but rarely is there an offer of anything new. A chapter dedicated to the case in a long-retired detective's memoir fleshes out a few tidbits, but nothing too close to the truth. It is a surprisingly good book, but that particular chapter is more conjecture than reality. A new wrinkle is the occasional true-crime podcast promising "new information" or a "huge break" in the case. Again, all bullshit.

The only people, as far as I know, on the face of the planet who knew the real story have never spoken a word of it. For good reason. And now, they are all gone. Except me.

As I walk through the door, I am greeted by the unmistakable scent of Dawson Brothers Funeral Home, which I have always figured to be a mix of freshly cut flowers, embalming fluid, and the musty wood of the creaky old building. Or maybe it's the ghosts.

A pasty ghoul in a black suit, purple dress shirt, and black tie, who looks like he is twenty-five and eighty-five years old at the same time, waves me towards the sparsely populated main room. It is an unnecessary gesture as Hound is the only act on the bill, but I suppose the young/old man figures he would not be doing his job if he does not direct each new patron straight towards the suffering.

I see some familiar faces dotting the room. Hound's Uncle Jimmy, his only remaining close family member, approaches as I grab a prayer card from the wooden stand and shove it in my pocket. The last time I had seen Uncle Jimmy was six years prior in this very same room when his sister Mary Ellen, Hound's mother, had passed away. At that time Jimmy looked like he was going to drop over and his half dozen or so remaining teeth were threatening to fall out of his head at any moment.

Jimmy is now around seventy and looks at least eighty, but by some miracle, a good eighty. Somehow healthy. And somewhere along the line he has gained a mouth full of teeth that would make a television evangelist jealous.

"Mickey Walsh, Esquire! Holy hell. I haven't seen you since I don't know when."

As Jimmy shakes my hand, tears well up in his eyes and I am compelled to bring him in for a hug.

"It's been a minute, Jimmy. You look good."

He backhands a tear from his cheek, manages a smile, and shakes his head.

"Thanks, brother. I have five years in. No booze. No weed or pills. I even stopped cigarettes a couple of years ago. I just wish Andrew never would have inherited the gene."

"Well, at least he had a couple of months sober before he got sick, Jim. Listen man, we both know Andy evaded the grim reaper a few times over the years."

He looks past me and absently nods at someone across the room.

"Yeah. We all have our stuff, you know what I mean, Mickey? But Andrew, he always had a hard time letting things go. I don't know what he was wrestlin' with all those years, but it finally won."

"Well, he was doing pretty well until the cancer hit him. Right?"

"Yeah, I mean he was sober as a judge when he got sick. Well, like you said, he had been clean for a little while, a couple months. Maybe it would have taken this time. But that damn lung cancer, you know, and all the drugs and booze and who knows what else, that all caught up to him. That, and I don't know, man. He just could never be happy long term, you know? He couldn't get no peace."

I nod in agreement because Uncle Jimmy speaks volumes. Hound could never find peace with himself or the world around him, whether he was clean or using, seeing a therapist, going to meetings. All of it helped, but none of it could make him forget.

"You were good to him, Jim. More like a big brother than an uncle."

Jimmy's eyes well up again and he hugs me hard, patting me on the back, unable to speak.

Words aren't necessary. Andrew Bassett had been the product of an on and off relationship between Mary Ellen and an irredeemable piece of trash by the name of something-or-other Bassett. The first name escapes me, and it really doesn't matter. They made a run at marriage, but Bassett didn't take very well to fatherhood, or marriage for that matter, so after three years, they divorced, predictably, and the guy moved out of state. He had not once tried to contact his son before getting killed in a six car pile-up on the Ohio Turnpike when Hound was nine years old.

So, despite his own demons, Jimmy had done his best to give Hound some semblance of a normal upbringing. A stranger might look at the two of them and figure he had failed. There was no white picket fence. No scrubbed up Sears family portrait tucked into a Christmas card with an accompanying letter about the previous year's achievements. There would be no glowing eulogy about all of Hound's business conquests. But under all the dysfunction and addiction, there was love. Hound always knew, even on his darkest day, he had family, albeit small, and he had a couple of good friends. And that is something.

To shake himself out of his crying fit, Jimmy flashes me a giant, artificial, toothy grin, and says, "Hey Walsh, what do you think of the choppers? Nice, huh?"

I shake my head and say, "You're ready to anchor the six o'clock news, Jimmy."

As I walk away, I hear him saying, "Yeah, brought to you by the kind folks at the University of Pittsburgh School of Dental Medicine."

It turns out Hound isn't in a box, but in an urn on a pedestal. Next to his remains on an easel is a recent photograph, enlarged and framed, of Hound in a sleeveless black t-shirt, head shaved, goatee, looking contemplative, or pensive, or maybe just constipated. If he could talk, Hound would say, "Holy crap! That picture's so big it should be strapped to the top of a black sedan in one of them commie parades." And he would be correct.

I chit-chat with some people from the old neighborhood, make hollow promises to get together, nod at the young/old hobgoblin in the hallway, then make my way back through the white door into the breeze. Sun has set and the light of day is hanging on by a thread.

As I take in all the sounds and smells of the neighborhood, I think about our carefree and fearless childhood days on these streets. Four boys who had each other's backs. Four boys who had promised they would protect each other no matter what. Four boys who had promised each other that the last man standing would tell the story. Three of those boys took that promise to the grave. First Bobby "Capone" DeLoretto. Then Frankie Kenney. Now Andrew "Hound" Bassett. Some might say they are all gone too young. Maybe Bobby and Frankie, but most would agree that Hound had outlived the odds. And I'm still here. The last man standing.

It's time to tell the story.

***

We were a hodge-podge crew, the four of us. Thrown together by the sheer luck of being drafted onto the same youth league baseball team. Arthur's Men's Shoppe. There were cooler teams, better teams, like the American Legion, or Sully's Tavern. But Art did offer a 20% discount to the boys on the team, which came in handy at Christmas when you had to buy your old man some new socks or a pack of t-shirts or the like.

When we were eleven, Bobby DeLoretto's dad went out for a pack of smokes and never returned. If Andrew Bassett's father hauling ass was as predictable as the sun coming up, Bobby's old man leaving was a shock to almost everybody. Almost. So, Bobby, who had diligently put aside a percentage of his paper route money all year with the intention of buying his old man a three pack of Fruit of the Loom boxers, used his discount to buy himself a fedora. Rumor had it that Art felt so bad about Bobby's pops skipping town, he gave him an extra 30% off on the hat. The fedora became as much a part of Bobby as his contempt for his dead-beat, absent old man, earning him the nickname "Capone."

If you would have lined up our whole team, Bobby would have been the last, or second to last guy you would pick if you had to guess which one of us had an old man who ran off (allegedly) with a twenty-two year old waitress from the Wagon Wheel Pancake House. From the outside looking in, Bobby's family was the picture of normalcy. He and his two older sisters were all at the top of the class, never missed school, and were always going to the library or museum and what not. His mother was a maternity ward nurse and she volunteered at the church bingo every Saturday night. His old man had used the G.I. Bill to get a college degree and worked as a sales manager for some big widget company out in the suburbs.

That's the thing, though. You never know what is really going on in a house unless you're on the inside. Apparently, pops had majored in business administration but had minored in philandering. He also, as it turned out, had a real problem with playing the ponies, and owed some pretty scary folks a mountain of money. Capone figured that debt had a lot to do with the old man skipping out. Well, that and the allure of a new life with the twenty-two year old waitress from the Wagon Wheel Pancake House.

Capone remained at the top of the class after his father left. In fact, he hit the books even harder. But we could see him getting a little more rebellious, a little quicker to anger, and a little more eager to mix it up if someone started in on him. And that was okay with us. It was an edge he had needed for a long time. Since he was still razor-sharp and getting straight A's, when he'd get in a little dust up, the Mercy nuns in grade school and eventually the Christian Brothers in high school could never point at a paltry grade point average and give him the old "You're a disappointment Mr. DeLoretto. It would be nice to see what you could do if you only applied yourself."

He was an enigma.

Frankie Kenney, on the other hand, actually *had* been raised in a family that was as close to normal as it got in our neighborhood. His living situation was out of the ordinary, but he had a mother and a father who loved each other and their two kids. They minded their own business and went about their lives without making waves. They were what we might call "under the radar" these days.

Frankie's family lived on the ground floor of a ten unit apartment building. Not in an apartment, but in an honest to goodness house with four bedrooms, full living and dining rooms, a kitchen and two big bathrooms, and their own entrance on the side of the building. They lived in this house within an apartment building because Frankie's dad was the superintendent of the ABC Apartments on the Boulevard. The three buildings, called Alice, Beverly, and Cecelia, after the original developer's daughters, took up an entire city block and in those days still held much of the stately charm they had when they were built in the late 1800's.

Frankie had been tagging along with his dad on calls from tenants to repair faulty wiring, unclog bathtubs and solve lock problems since he was a toddler. Hence, Frankie could fix anything. Bike chains, baseball gloves, gas mowers. His patience and ability to make things work like new seemingly had no boundary. He had also painted nearly every inch of Alice, Beverly, and Cecelia's interiors at least once. When a unit was between tenants, Frankie and his older brother Thomas (Not Tom or Tommy, but Thomas. Who knows why.) would roll in with their dad and clean the place, then paint every wall in every room. Eggshell white. No time to differentiate between baseboards and walls. Nothing fancy. And never any color but eggshell white.

By the time Frankie was ten and Thomas thirteen, they were on their own with the cleaning and painting. They were fast, efficient, and neat. Never a drop on the hardwood floors.

And me? Well, I was bread and buttered, as they say, in a large Irish Catholic household which consisted of nine kids, two worn out parents, and a grandmother thrown into the mix when I was six for good measure. I am the second to last child of five girls and four boys. It was all pretty standard, really. Don't leave the table until you finish your plate. Don't lollygag in the bathroom. Don't tarnish the family name at school. And by all means, don't wake your parents up with a phone call from the police station in the middle of the night. Now that I think about it, the last one happened three times over twenty years, and that was three times more than any of those other three things happened. Life is strange that way.

And Joseph Robert Bertram? Well, none of us had ever laid eyes on him in the flesh. But when the nine year old boy had gone missing in the spring of 1977 it was all over the news and in the papers for months. He had last been accounted for in a corner store on his way home from school in Brookline, a neighborhood that was as foreign to us as the Amazon or the Australian Outback. From our neighborhood, you had to cross a river and go through a tunnel to get to Brookline. Most people who made that trip only did it once. And that was when they moved to the south hills for greener pastures. Or maybe they did it reluctantly a few times a year to visit those relatives who had made the move. One thing is for certain. Once they returned, there would be a lot of bitching and complaining about tunnel traffic and how there was no easy way to get there or back again. My dad had a theory that some people went there with no intention of moving, but just stayed because it was easier than sitting in bumper to bumper traffic in the Liberty Tunnels, breathing in exhaust fumes on the way home.

So, Bertram wasn't part of our crew, but his disappearance cast a long shadow over us, and kids all over the city. We were all on high alert. We were street smart, and leery of creeps and strangers anyway, but we were wise enough to know if it could happen to a kid in Brookline in broad daylight, it could happen to any of us.

Spring rolled into summer, and every day there was a new report of a lead on the six o'clock news on all three channels and in both papers. A car had been seen creeping around the area. A shady trio of teens had been in the store not long before Bertram. A so-called psychic from some faraway place had shown up at the Public Safety Building downtown with information she had garnered in a vision. None of it led anywhere.

After a couple of months, coverage had tapered to a weekly update and a recurring plea from police for anyone with information to step forward.

Also, that summer, the ABC apartments had seen an unprecedented rash of departures. Eight units in the three buildings were vacated for various reasons. Luckily, demand for the apartments was high and the void would be filled by autumn. But Mr. Kenney's cleaning and painting crew had been cut in half because Thomas (not Tom or Tommy) had a summer filled with science camps, scout jamborees, and a prolonged and reluctant stay with relatives in Altoona.

In order to make up for the gaping hole in his work force, Mr. Kenney enlisted the help of me and Hound, under the supervision of Frankie, to clean and paint the eight units. Child labor laws be damned. We were happy to do it. He paid cash every Friday, and Mrs. Kenney made us lunch every day. Life was good. Capone, who had an extremely large and lucrative paper route, wanted no part of being bossed around by Frankie Kenney all summer, so he passed. In hindsight, he could have done both jobs because he spent most of his time in the apartments watching us work and shooting the breeze.

According to Mr. Kenney, Myrna Stevens had lived in Apartment 1D on the first floor of Cecelia since "the dawn of man." In July of '77 her apartment was penciled in as our ninth and final project after she fell asleep in her La-Z-Boy recliner while watching The Price is Right and never woke up. Considering the fact that she had lived in the place since the Hoover administration (true fact), we fully expected her unit to be a challenge. But as luck would have it, Myrna was a neat freak, a germaphobe, and had the simple living habits of a cloistered nun. Aside from a bottomless bowl of butterscotch candies and a voluminous, alphabetized wall of hardback books, her near-pristine apartment consisted of next to nothing. She had no family, had outlived all her friends, and according to Mr. Kenney, until the day she died had been the most consistently happy tenant in the three buildings. For me, Hound and Frankie, this meant one trip to the dumpster, one trip to the curb, all the butterscotch we wanted, and exponentially less cleaning than any of the other units we had refreshed that summer.

We were putting the finishing touches on Myrna's apartment and were down to our last five gallon bucket of eggshell white, when our lives were forever changed in one afternoon.

***

Frankie dipped his brush into the can and wiped the excess off one side before running it perfectly down the wall along the door frame.

"Hey, did you guys see Elvis from Alice-3C yesterday? It looks like he broke his arm."

"Is that Fat Elvis or Jailhouse Rock Elvis?" asked Capone.

We had nicknames for every tenant in the ABC Apartments and every neighborhood character. Especially the odd-ball, larger than life neighborhood characters.

Jailhouse Rock Elvis was maybe twenty-five years old, but unlike most young guys in 1977, he had the full greaser look going. Always walking around like he was on his way to a rumble or a drag race in 1959. Fat Elvis was old. Older than real Elvis, but he had the same haircut and those gaudy gold glasses with fake jewels on them. Word was Fat

Elvis was somehow connected to the mob. We figured that was just a load of crap someone made up on account of the Elvis glasses. To us he was just another schlub working his way through life. He was the guy who came and got the money out of the vending and pinball machines at every pizza joint and store in the neighborhood.

"That's Jailhouse Rock Elvis," Frankie said. "Fat Elvis lives in Cecelia. He comes at you in smell-o-vision, that guy. I hope I'm long gone before he vacates his apartment."

I shook my head and winced. "So how did Jailhouse Elvis break his arm?"

"Beats me, but he has a black eye too," Frankie said.

Hound peeked his head in from the hallway and said, "I seen him yesterday out on the corner. He says he fell at work, but he clearly got his ass kicked."

"How do you know that?" I asked.

"Well, I seen his big cast so of course I had to ask him what happened, and he got all squirrely and tells me he fell. I didn't call him on it because he was all jumpy about it. Plus, if I was him and I got my ass kicked, I wouldn't be telling some little kid about it."

Capone waved his hat towards Hound and said, "You're not a little kid, Hound, you're just vertically challenged, and also woefully underweight for your age."

Hound, who had yet to even sniff a growth spurt, was used to the jokes.

"Funny Capone, funny. You ever thought about going on the road with that act? I'll buy you the bus ticket."

Capone and Hound would go at each other relentlessly, but they had an unwritten pact. No mentions of absent fathers. Ever. Even before Capone's old man took off, none of us ever went down that road with Hound. Some things are sacred.

Along with Elvis and Elvis, the apartment complex had plenty of characters. Myrna, who didn't need a nickname, because, well, she was an old lady named Myrna. And Barney Fife in Beverly, who looked nothing like Don Knotts, but took his job as security officer at the hospital way too seriously. There was Ringo in Alice 3-A, who was always playing his drums in the middle of the day for the whole neighborhood to hear. And Laurie, whose real name was Margie, looked just like Susan Dey, so obviously we called her Laurie, as in Laurie Partridge. We had Sloth in Beverly 1-B who looked and moved like a tree sloth in a three piece suit.

A new addition to the list was a tall, skinny, forty-something guy who had moved into the apartment across from Myrna in early 1977. He kept to himself, had a pencil-thin mustache and parted his short hair not quite in the middle, but not quite on the side either. An odd look for 1977. Capone, who was somewhat of a classic movie buff, had dubbed him "The Thin Man." Naturally, none of us knew where he came up with that nickname, so he explained.

"You guys have never seen the movie The Thin Man? That guy is a dead ringer for William Powell, who played The Thin Man. And his co-star was Myrna Loy, just like our dearly departed Myrna. Bonus points."

Hound shook his head and said, "Yeah Capone, we're not seventy. We don't spend our days going to bingo and watching movies from the freakin' nineteen-thirties like you apparently do."

"Whatever, man. Take my word for it. It's perfect."

Capone had never steered us wrong with a nickname, so we rolled with it.

The Thin Man never spoke to us in the few days we were working in Myrna's apartment. We'd see him come and go, pass him in the hall, nod, say hello, but we'd never get anything back. He'd look down, rarely make eye contact, and rush by us.

As Hound swept the hallway, I washed my hands in the kitchen sink, and Capone, legs crossed, sat on a wooden chair flipping through the morning newspaper like an old man on a park bench. Come to think of it, maybe Hound was on to something.

Frankie turned after deftly putting the finishing touches on Myrna's wall, and said, "No sandwiches today fellas. My mother had to go downtown for something."

Hound, in mock anger said, "Jesus, Frank! Tell her to get her ass back here and make us lunch!"

Frankie waved his brush towards Hound and said, "Have no fear, moocher, she gave me money. We can walk over to Lenny's for a pizza."

"All is right with the world," said Capone, "God forbid Hound has to part with any of his communion money!"

So off we went, across the Boulevard, down a couple of streets, and through a few shortcut alleys to the best (and cheapest) pie in the neighborhood at Lenny's Nearly Famous Pizza and Pasta.

***

We returned to Cecelia an hour or so later and as we walked through the front door, we could hear the muffled sound of conversation, not an unusual occurrence in an apartment building. But as we stepped through the vestibule and into the stark hallway, the voices bouncing off the walls while still unintelligible, were urgent and heightened.

The four of us remained silent, stopping in our tracks. The conversation between the two men, one pleading, the other calm, but fierce and angry, was coming from The Thin Man's apartment.

Capone scooped up a tattered piece of paper that lay on the floor.

Turning it over he said, "HOLY CRAP! Guys, look at this!"

In his hands was a police sketch, the kind we had all seen in the movies and on TV a million times. But it was real. Very real. At the top of the paper in bold print were the words POLICE DEPARTMENT – CITY of NEW YORK. Below the drawing were some particulars on the suspect and a synopsis of his alleged crimes.

But what drew us to the page was the charcoal sketch.

Capone asked, "Who does this look like to you guys?"

"I don't know, Bobby. Who's it supposed to look like?" I asked, knowing full well what he was getting at.

Capone said, "Is it just me or does this look like The Thin Man?"

Hound leaned in and took a good, long look. "Maybe. 'Stache looks the same, but I don't know."

Frankie shook his head and said, "The 'stache and that weird no man's land part in his hair. I mean who has that going on these days?"

The voices continued, one remaining calm and fierce and the other escalating to desperation.

Without thinking of the potential consequences and for reasons he would never be able to explain, Hound opened the door of The Thin Man's apartment and walked into the living room, the rest of us pleading with him not to do it.

Looking through the arched doorway into the dining room, he saw the back of a large man in a leather jacket, obscuring the other man who sat in a chair at the table. The large man bent towards the pleading, desperate man and without hesitation or difficulty, choked the life out of him. Later, when Hound was finally able to string some words together about it, he said the big man did it like it was nothing. Like he had done it a thousand times before.

Hound's mouth agape, his barely audible gasp caused the big man to turn and draw a pistol from inside his jacket. Waving it at Hound, he said, "Don't move. Don't go nowhere."

Frankie, Capone, and I could see Hound through the open door of the apartment but did not at that point know exactly what he had witnessed, but we knew he was too scared to move a muscle. He had also pissed his pants and was shaking like a leaf. We knew whatever had just taken place in that apartment was serious and horrible and not like anything else he had ever seen.

The three of us never had the urge to run, scream, or do anything other than watch Hound through the doorway. We were all in a state of shock. We could hear heavy footsteps as the man approached Hound. We then saw him, gun in hand, as he said, "What are we gonna do here, kid?"

Hound, unable to speak, stood looking first up at the man then out into the hallway at us.

The man, seeing the three of us on the other side of the door, shook his head, muttered something, and waved us into the room.

At some point, the big man must have covered the dead man's body with a sheet. All we saw in the other room was a dingy green lump. Thank God.

He slowly walked over to the apartment door, closed and locked it, and turned towards the four of us.

"We have quite a situation here fellas. First of all, that guy under the sheet over there. He is a very bad man."

The four of us stood looking at a man who had just taken the life out of another man and heard him say the dead man was the bad guy. Even at twelve years old, I can clearly recall thinking that was going to take some explaining. Also, in that moment, who were we to argue?

He noticed the police sketch in Capone's hand and said, "See the guy in the drawing? That's him. Under the sheet."

That made sense. We had already bandied about the theory that the goon in the sketch was The Thin Man. And we were now in his apartment. And there was a dead guy under a sheet also in The Thin Man's apartment.

Capone, snapping out of the stupor, said, "So are you a cop? This drawing says New York on it."

"No. I'm not a cop. And there *will be* no cops involved in this, understand? Not now. Not ever."

He directed us all to sit on a shabby couch in the living room and disappeared into the dining room, returning with a shoebox.

"This greasy son of a bitch killed my nephew about a year ago, but only after doing unspeakable things to him. My sister's only son. That was in New York City. Queens. They found his body buried under a bridge. Nine years old."

His face reddened and we could see the rage and grief building in him as he spoke. I recall feeling a sense of relief at that moment, knowing even though this hulk of a man had just killed a person with his bare hands, he had no interest in killing four twelve year old boys.

Capone spoke again, asking, "How do you know it was him? I mean we're in Pittsburgh and that happened in New York."

He stared an icy hole through Capone and said, "Let's just say in my line of work, we have ways to find people."

We knew the sketch looked an awful lot like The Thin Man, and we knew we were sitting in The Thin Man's apartment on his crappy couch, so it added up.

"And another thing," he said, "This son of a bitch confessed to killing a kid here a couple of months ago. When I busted in on him, that's who he thought I was here about."

Frankie blurted out, "Bertram?"

"Yeah. That's him. Then he copped to a few more when he was bargaining for his life."

"So, why not call the police? Why do, well, that?" I asked, waving at the green lump in the other room.

He looked at me hard but had thawed a bit, realizing he would have to give us some context for what had just happened.

"And let that animal live in prison until he dies an old man? No. Not after what he did to Lorenzo. Or these other kids. Justice was done swiftly."

It went against everything I had learned, but I'd be lying if I said I didn't see where he was coming from.

Frankie asked, "So what's your line of work? How do you find people? Are you a private eye?"

"Let's just say I dispose of, um, problems for a certain type of organization."

Hound shot up as if he had just been awakened by a bucket of ice cold water, and said, "You're a freakin' hitman! Holy crap!"

"Listen. You said that, not me. But there lies the rub. I am here of my own accord. Nobody sent me here to do this job. And if this gets out, it will be a very unpleasant problem for me from all sides. Get it?"

I said, "No. What do you mean?"

"Meaning it would be bad for me if anyone finds out I did this on my own. Anyone. The people I work for OR the police. Hence, nobody will speak of this again. Nobody. No telling anyone anything that happened here today. Or, and I hate to say this out loud, that could be bad for you."

"Jesus Christ!" Capone said. "We've been walking in and out of these buildings all summer with this guy living right here."

Capone had come right up to the doorstep, but he had not stated the obvious. A mafia hitman may have saved one of us from being The Thin Man's next victim. As uneasy, terrified, and shaken as we were, we all knew this was not a stretch.

We also knew a not so veiled threat from a contract killer was enough to seal the fact that what we had seen and heard that day would go no further than the people in that room. Ever. But our friend needed a little insurance.

"I need all your names. No bullshit. No games. And here is the deal. You need to know that just the way I found that piece of filth in the other room, I, and my associates, have ways to find you and anyone else if it becomes necessary. And we need to keep each other and the people we love safe. Am I clear?"

Crystal. We needed no arm twisting to realize he meant business. We had evidence he would kill. We knew he had no interest in hurting us, but we also knew he had no interest in prison or being taken out by his own. We also knew he had relieved the world of a very bad man that day.

He, on the other hand, knew, even though we were four very frightened children, we had some leverage in the deal.

After we had dutifully given him our names, I spoke up, "So, what's your name? We gave you ours. It's only fair, you know, so we can make sure you hold up your end. We have a lot to lose here by not going to the police."

"Sorry kid. I can't do that. You'll just have to trust me. And I will be checking in with you."

I didn't know it at the time, but that exchange had earned me the position of point person for the group. A position I would hold for the next few decades. Although he wouldn't give up his name, it had turned out to be rather easy to figure out. By the time we had encountered him that day, Nicholas "Ray-Ray" Raymondi had already begun to garner a reputation as a very prolific man in his chosen profession. Over the decades, the reputation grew, and we had gotten accustomed to seeing him on the national news. Always around the action. Implicated in several hits, but never convicted. He would even go on to be the basis for a character in a blockbuster mob movie that had been "based on true events."

The big man gestured in the general direction of the dining room, and said, "Okay, so now I gotta take care of the rest of this, so you need to go. I don't care where, but just go. I realize this is a lot and I sincerely wish you didn't get involved, but it is what it is. And remember, never a word."

With that, we went across the hall to Myrna's and sat mostly in silence for the rest of the afternoon.

Our new friend was out of The Thin Man's apartment within an hour, leaving no trace of himself, The Thin Man, or a murder. He left a neatly written note from Randall Lee Hatcher (aka The Thin Man) explaining why he had to abruptly move out of state for an immediate employment opportunity. Along with the letter was the next three months' rent in cash that he had "hoped would make up for any trouble" his abrupt departure would cause.

Randall Lee Hatcher, we eventually surmised, must have been alone in the world or at the very least estranged from any family, because from that day to this one, he has never been reported as missing. On that day, he ceased to exist, and no member of the human race seemed to care.

After a few days of letting things process, the four of us met at the pizza shop and entered an agreement that never really had to be spoken. But we formalized it anyway.

Capone, who had always had a way of putting things in context said, "It's like that Japanese statue of the three wise monkeys."

"Jesus, Capone! You're going to have to give us more than that," Frankie said.

"You know. See no evil, hear no evil, speak no evil. We have to go about life like we never saw anything, never heard anything, and we sure as hell can never speak of this again."

We all agreed. Time passed and we kept our word. We never mentioned that day again. It was not as if it had never happened. On the contrary, that day had shaped all four of our lives. But on the surface, we all went on as best we could as if it had never happened.

***

When Nicholas "Ray-Ray" Raymondi said he had ways to find people, he was not exaggerating. Over the decades, even as his "fame" grew, he would check in with me to make sure everyone was still aware of our deal and the possible ramifications of breaching said deal. Years would go by, and the messages were often cryptic, but the point was made.

On some level, we felt we owed it to Ray-Ray to move on. The Thin Man was a monster. A monster who never had the opportunity to hurt a little kid again. A monster who never had the opportunity to kill again.

Capone, who had done a couple of years in the Army to pay for college, had stayed in the reserves after his stint and became one of the first casualties of the Gulf War when he and about a dozen other soldiers from his unit were killed in a missile attack. He left a wife and a toddler behind.

Frankie Kenney had moved out of the neighborhood a year after the "incident" when his father had taken a job as director of maintenance for a big hospital out in the suburbs. After not seeing him for over a decade, he appeared at Capone's memorial service and from that day until he died, we had remained close friends. He had married his high school sweetheart, had three kids, and went on to be quite successful in commercial real estate. Frankie died of a heart attack on a golf course in Florida at the age of fifty, just three months after running his eleventh marathon. You just never know.

***

And then there is the fifth member of our exclusive club, Nicholas "Ray-Ray" Raymondi, reputed mafia hitman and actual exterminator of Randall Lee Hatcher. Ray-Ray is what you might call an enigma. Documentarians, informants, and countless pixelated faces, silhouettes, and altered voices over the years had anointed him the most prolific contract killer in American history. Yet, when Capone passed away, he sent me a very sincere sympathy card and called me directly to offer condolences when Frankie had died. I've always theorized that it was Ray-Ray who had anonymously loaded Capone's son's college fund with enough money to cover an Ivy League education and had done the same for the three Kenney children upon Frankie's death. I can't prove that, but I'd bet my house on it.

About a month before Andrew Bassett had ended up in the gentle care of the Dawson Brothers Funeral Home, I had received a call from Ray-Ray's assistant summoning me to Las Vegas. In all the years since we had made our deal with this enigmatic devil, he had never asked me to meet him in person. There had been an ebb and flow of cautious and vague messages from him, but never a request for a one on one meeting. I thought it strange, but also felt the pull of four and a half decades of nearly unbearable secrecy drawing me to the desert for a face-to-face with Raymondi. I was also aware that Hound was in his final lap, and it was likely I would be the last of the four of us very soon.

Twelve hours after that call, I was on a direct overnight flight from Pittsburgh to Vegas packed with eager gamblers, two bachelorette parties, and a handful of business types. And then there was me. I had been to Vegas probably twenty times, mostly for conventions and seminars, but never for a meeting with a contract killer. That part was new.

After a loud but otherwise uneventful flight, I navigated the slot machines and hustle and bustle of travelers at the gates and in the concourses of the frenetic airport to the ride share pick-up area. Once there I was whisked away not by an Uber or a Lyft, but by a guy named Vinnie, straight out of central casting, in a black SUV that had been sent by Ray-Ray.

Heading west away from the strip and into the ever-growing desert suburban sprawl, Vinnie and I made thirty minutes of small talk, mostly about the weather ("Dry heat, my ass. It is still hot as balls out here."), hockey ("These are great fans, but nobody out here understands the blue line."), his boyhood in Brooklyn ("I go back twice a year just for the meatballs."), and his recent pleasant encounter in line at the pharmacy with "Penn or Teller, whichever one don't talk."

We ended up in Summerlin, an expansive development of homes on land once purchased for a song by Howard Hughes and named for his mother. After meandering through a couple of streets lined with near-identical tan, stucco houses, a garage door opened as if it had been waiting for us, and the SUV was swallowed into the belly of a house that was nearly indistinguishable from any other house on the street.

As we entered the kitchen from the garage, Vinnie shook my hand, thanked me for the "good talk," and dismissed himself through the front door. A tall, slightly hunched man emerged from the darkness of a hallway on the other end of the open floor plan. As he moved closer, I could see it was Ray-Ray, but he was a mere shadow of the man who had choked the life out of The Thin Man so many years earlier. I hadn't seen Ray-Ray in person since our fateful day, but I had seen his career play out on the screen over the past forty-five years, and this was a man, like Hound, who was not long for this world.

"Mickey. I appreciate you coming all the way out here."

His voice was thin and weak, and his signature wave of salt and pepper hair was gone. His olive skin had given way to a pale gray, and he wore sweatpants that probably cost more than my flight. He topped off the look with a Vegas Golden Knights golf shirt that was at this point two or three sizes too big.

He motioned me towards a surprisingly minimal dining room table and said, "Sit. This won't take long, but it must be done in person."

He shuffled over to the refrigerator and grabbed two bottles of water before joining me at the table.

The shoebox that Ray-Ray had emerged from The Thin Man's room with on that day in 1977 sat on the table, sealed in a large, clear, plastic bag.

He gestured towards the shoebox and said, "I'll get to this in a minute. The others, do you hear from their widows or children? And your friend Andrew? How is he?"

I assessed Ray-Ray, not knowing whether he knew of Hound's illness or was just asking in general and said, "Andrew's dying. Lung Cancer. I saw him the other day and to be honest I don't think he has much time."

Ray-Ray looked genuinely saddened by this news, shook his head and said, "Jesus, that's too bad. It really is. It must be going around, the lung cancer. Same thing here. It was stage four before I even knew what it was. Moved to who the hell knows where else. Now there are spots on my brain. I never even smoked."

He stared beyond me, but there seemed to be no fear, no remorse, no emotion at all in his eyes.

"Anyway, I got nothing left. The tank's empty. I'm done with treatment and every day it gets harder to get out of bed. I got maybe a month or two."

His hands were still wide and strong, but attached now to a skinny, failing body. His face held the cheekbones of a once large and imposing man, and his cauliflower ears dwarfed his bald head.

I felt the same pity for him as I would any person who was dying a harsh death, but it was tempered by the thought that this is the price he pays for the life he had lived. I had no doubt if I were to articulate that out loud, he would agree.

I said, "I'm sorry to hear that. It's not an easy thing to go through, I'm sure. And yes, I keep in touch with Capone and Frankie's families. It was thoughtful, what you did. The college funds."

He smirked, waved it off, and sighed.

"I don't know what you're talking about. And this shitty disease, well, it is what it is. I hope your friend Andrew has a peaceful time of it."

With that he gestured towards the shoebox and said, "This box... "

I interrupted, "I remember it from that day."

He chuckled again and said, "You have a good memory, but then again, I am sure that is a day you have never forgotten."

"I remember every detail, for better or for worse."

"Then you remember that I said that piece of filth confessed to me that he had killed the Bertram boy from Pittsburgh, and he also mentioned others?"

"I do remember that, yes."

He unleashed a sandy dry cough and took a sip of water. He gave himself a minute to regroup, then tapped his large, middle finger on the table.

"Well, in that box is evidence of every killing. His type, they like to take souvenirs, and he was no different, the sick bastard."

He looked me in the eye, shook his head in disappointment, and said, "I've taken a lot of people out of this world. I know what I am. I have no delusions or reservations about that. None of the men I took out were altar boys. But Hatcher, he was the worst of the lot. Other than you and your friends getting caught in that mess, if I had a thousand chances to choke that bastard out, I'd do it every time and then once more. My one other regret, though, is that those kids, their families, they never got the closure they deserve."

Ray-Ray had probably never been so straightforward about the life he had lived. But he had nothing on the line. He once again gestured towards the shoebox and said, "You and your friends kept your end of the deal. You were just kids when this went down, and what you all did was not easy. And I appreciate that. I ain't gonna tell you what to do."

He snickered at the absurdity of his statement.

"I'll be freakin' dead anyway, but you know what I mean. What I'm saying is, I have sort of a last wish and I am hoping you can fulfill it once I am dead."

He went over his wishes in detail and when he was satisfied that I was ready for the assignment, America's most prolific contract killer and I spent the rest of the afternoon on his back patio watching over the hill golfers miss putt after putt on a green that sat maybe forty feet from his seldom-used in-ground pool. It was the second most surreal day of my life.

Nicholas "Ray-Ray" Raymondi had the courtesy to die two days before Andrew "Hound" Bassett. His death, while newsworthy, did not make near the splash it would have made in his prime. He had predicted this as we sat on the patio that day watching a loudmouth old man miss a three foot gimme with an eight hundred dollar putter.

"Once I am gone, do what I've asked."

***

I take a seat on a well-worn barstool in Sully's Tavern, just around the corner from Dawson Brothers' Funeral Home and order an Iron City.

As the bartender hunches over to pop open the bottle, he nods over his shoulder towards the flat screen on the wall.

"You see this?"

Joseph Bertram's school picture is on the screen among a montage of six other young boys on the left and the artist's sketch of The Thin Man on the right. I can't hear the report, but I can see the closed captioning scrolling at the bottom of the screen.

The bartender, at least ten years my senior, places the beer on a coaster and shakes his head in amazement.

"Out of nowhere the FBI gets a package with a box of souvenirs from a serial killer who murdered the kid from Brookline way back in 1977, and it looks like a bunch of other kids all over the place."

He is now dunking pilsner glasses in that magic blue water and placing them on a shelf below the bar.

"And get a load of this! He was living right over on the Boulevard in one of those apartment buildings, the triplets, and just took a powder one day."

I look as wide eyed as I can at him and say, "Wow, that is unbelievable!"

"Hey, you're Walsh, right? Michael."

"Yeah, Mickey."

The gears turn and I try to place him, but he beats me to it.

"Donny Zulenski. My sister Nancy was about your age, right?"

"Yeah, maybe two years older than me. Wow, good memory."

"Yeah, I remember a lot of useless shit. You ran around with the kid who lived in the triplets, right? Kenney?"

"Right, Frankie. He died a little while back. In fact, that whole crew is gone. I was just at Andrew Bassett's viewing at Dawsons."

"Yeah, his Uncle Jimmy is a buddy of mine. He doesn't come in anymore, and believe me, that's for the best. Sorry about your friend."

"Thanks. He was a good guy. A survivor."

He stands upright and wags a finger towards me. I know what's coming, so I beat him to it.

"Yeah, we spent a lot of time in those buildings back in the day. We were even working with Frankie that summer. Crazy. Hearing this is scary. This monster was right there the whole time!"

He nods and I continue to play dumb.

"How'd this package end up with the FBI anyway?"

"Holy shit! Here's the craziest part. Turns out one of the dead kids from New York was some mafia hitman's nephew or something. The hitman just died in Vegas a few days ago and lo and behold, this package lands at an FBI field office with a whole document he wrote outlining the whole thing. He goes on and on about feeling bad for all these kids and their families. So far it all checks out. It's like some damn movie stuff! You can't make this shit up."

"You don't say! So, what happened to the serial killer?"

This part, genuinely has me on pins and needles. Obviously, I know the truth, but Ray-Ray, at his dining room table, had refused to detail what he had written.

"The hitman, in the document, says he connected enough dots to figure out who killed his nephew, tracked the guy to Pittsburgh. Said he never even considered involving law enforcement because they had, get this, a 'strained relationship.' No shit. Drove overnight from New York City, knocked right on the guy's door, kidnapped him at gunpoint, and then drove him all the way back to Jersey, where he strangled him and buried him in the middle of nowhere. Like some Jimmy Hoffa-type shit!"

"That's insane!" I try my best not to overdo the surprise.

Ray-Ray had never given us any indication of what he had done after ordering us out of The Thin Man's apartment that day, and we never wanted to know. I am relieved to hear he took some artistic license and let on that he killed Hatcher somewhere other than in the apartment.

"I can't believe that! How did he get the guy out of there undetected in broad daylight?"

"Good question. But he claimed he didn't see another soul in the buildings and never spoke to another person other than the serial killer the whole trip! He even called it the perfect hit. Crazy, right?"

He turns to the flatscreen as the coverage switches to a live aerial shot of police and an excavation crew somewhere in Jersey digging deep holes in a remote field in search of the remains of Randall Lee Hatcher, aka The Thin Man.

I finish my beer, settle up with my new friend Donny, and head back out into the now cooler, crisp, late summer air.

The same wind chime makes soft music, and I am struck by the thought that Capone, Frankie, and Hound had all died with our pact intact, never knowing Ray-Ray had written an unlikely final chapter to our strange story.

Or, I think to myself, maybe they do know the end. Who really knows. As I approach my car I fumble in my pocket for the keys and pull out Hound's prayer card, looking at it for the first time. On one side I am not surprised to find the Serenity Prayer. On the other, under Andrew Bassett's name and pertinent dates, are two sentences in quotes, attributed to 'Anonymous.'

'My word was my bond. And now I am free.'

Ten bittersweet words. And not so anonymous. Of the four of us, our secret took the greatest toll on Hound. Somehow Capone, Frankie and I were able to wrestle with the moral aspects of keeping quiet about a murder and knowing the identity of a man who had killed a half dozen or so innocent boys. Perhaps we had rationalized that even though it was sad and maybe even cruel that there were families out there still searching, still hoping their sons and brothers would walk through the door, Ray-Ray had rid the world of a monster.

That, and the fact that he may have saved one of us from harm, provided just enough rationale to allow us to move along in life without too much damage. There was also the fact that Ray-Ray killed people for a living and was damn good at it, seemingly with no remorse. We had theorized all along that he had no interest in eliminating us, but given his track record, it isn't a theory we had ever wanted to test.

But I figure because Hound was an eyewitness, he had carried the ordeal the way Jacob Marley wore those chains. But unlike Marley, with death, comes liberation. At least that's what I'm going with.

Thin clouds move quickly across the backdrop of pitch black, star filled sky. I take a long look up and down the block at the streets that formed me. It is different. Not just different in the way a place changes over time. I am different. The world is different. A heavy weight has been lifted, but I still feel a sense of loneliness.

I am the last man standing. I have told the story once and I will never tell it again. I like Ray-Ray's version better.

Acknowledgements

To my fellow Oaklanders, I raise a glass to you and to our unique neighborhood!

Dr. William Snyder helped me to harness my creative thoughts as a student at Saint Vincent College. These many years later, he continues to be a great source of encouragement. To Bill and all the educators in my life, I appreciate you.

Finally, I must thank my family, immediate and extended, past and present, for influencing me, teaching me, allowing me the space to be creative, and for being a never-ending source of inspiration.

***

To learn more and to join the author's mailing list, visit *patrickhalfertyauthor.com*.